Love and Other Lies

Karma Never Knocks

By Ann Winston

This is a work of fiction. Names, characters, businesses, places, events, and incidents are either the products of the author's imagination or used in a fictitious manner. Any resemblance to actual persons, living or dead or actual events is purely coincidental.

To my father, Samuel Winston. Thank you for your strength, courage, creativity, and unique sense of humor.

Table of Contents

ONE

"Felicia, he's awake..."

Felicia was so focused on sharing her decision, Dr. Walsh had to repeat himself.

"Felicia, did you hear me? Kenneth is awake."

"He's awake. Yes, I heard you. But how could he... why did he...this makes no sense."

Dr. Walsh was surprised by Felicia's lack of enthusiasm. "It happens sometimes. On rare occasions, and by some miracle, some people are able to regain consciousness. Of course, we won't know his brain activity until we've had time to run some tests."

Felicia could hear herself rambling, but couldn't control it. "So, he's back? I mean, is he back to stay?"

Dr. Walsh ran his fingers through his hair. "If you're asking if he'll remain awake, I can't give you an answer. Sometimes they drift in and out, then fall unconscious again. Other times, they make as close to a full recovery as can be expected. I'll know more in the next few days."

Felicia turned to the girls as if she was searching for her next steps. Carolyn nodded her head toward the door. Felicia picked up on her cue. "Can we see him?"

Dr. Walsh shook his head while preparing her for the visit. "Felicia you can go in for a few minutes, but I'm afraid other visitors could be too much excitement. Please know he's going to look and act very differently. His eyes can't focus, and he can't speak. We're not even sure he'll even recognize you. Speak softly and calmly. Are you ready?"

Felicia took a deep breath as the exes gave her supportive pats and smiles. "Yes, I'm ready."

Felicia thought she was moving forward but she hadn't taken a step. Dr. Walsh was well into the room before he realized Felicia wasn't behind him.

"Felicia, are you coming?"

Felicia leaned back against the ladies.

"No. I wasn't prepared for...I'm not ready for..."

Carolyn immediately jumped into action.

"It's okay, you don't have to go in. It's really okay. Come over here and sit down."

With each step, Felicia relied more on the ladies to hold her up. They led her to the row of chairs across from the nurse's station, and as she plopped into the chair, her head fell into her hands. Carolyn squatted in front of her.

"Take a few deep breaths. Jessica, get her some water."

The sound of her name snapped Jessica out of her trance and she scurried off to get help from a nurse. Carolyn rose just enough to sit down beside Felicia and whispered, "Look, you're gonna drink a little water, and we're getting out of here. Let's all go back to your house and regroup. The last thing you need is a bunch of nosey nurses soaking up your every move for tonight's gossip."

Felicia shook her head in agreement, and began to rise. Carolyn supported her on one side, as they slowly moved toward the elevators. Jessica returned with the water just in time to see the elevator doors opening. She sat the water on the counter and scurried to catch up with the ladies.

Mitchell was standing in front of the window with Emmanuel in his arms. He was pointing to birds and squirrels, delighting Emmanuel with each new discovery. Felicia bolted from the elevator so quickly, When the elevator doors opened to the lobby, Mitchell hardly had time to turn around. His warm smile disappeared when he saw the expression on Felicia's face.

"What's wrong? What happened? Was he...gone?"

Felicia pulled Emmanuel from Mitchell's arms.

"No – he wasn't gone. As a matter of fact, he was very much alive. So much alive in fact, that he's awake!"

"What do you mean? I...don't understand. I thought he was..."

"On the brink of death? Damaged beyond repair? Yes, that's what I thought too! But apparently the word COMA doesn't mean what it used to!"

Mitchell was trying to keep up, but was failing miserably, so he looked toward Carolyn for clarification. Carolyn stepped up to the plate.

"We got up there and before Felicia could give them her decision, the doctor met us in the doorway and told us Kenneth was awake."

Mitchell bent over as if he'd been punched in the stomach. "What the..."

Carolyn and Jessica responded in harmony, "I KNOW!"

Mitchell quickly recovered, realizing he had to be strong for Felicia. "Oh, Sweetheart, let's get you home."

Felicia wasn't ready to put Emmanuel back in his chair, so Mitchell carried the empty seat to the car while Felicia found temporary comfort in nuzzling her cub.

Jessica yelled to Felicia that she'd be at the house shortly, but Felicia never looked back. She chose to focus on strapping in Emmanuel and let Mitchell confirm the plans.

Mitchell worked to get Emmanuel out of the car while Felicia unlocked the front door. She mumbled something to Mitchell about leaving the door unlocked for the girls, and made her way to the couch. Before she could get comfortable, she heard Carolyn and Jessica in the entry. Carolyn headed for Emmanuel while Jessica made her way to the bar and began mixing drinks. Felicia and Carolyn briefed Mitchell on the hospital visit while Emmanuel gnawed on Carolyn's chin. Mitchell sat slumped on the couch in disbelief. As hard as he tried, he couldn't help feeling a little selfish. He'd never say it, but Mitchell was disappointed that the day didn't end with some type of closure. He tried to pose a question that didn't appear to be completely self-serving.

"So, what did the doctor say about a game plan for Kenneth? What happens next?"

Carolyn turned to answer, but Felicia beat her to it.

"I don't know. We didn't get that far. I was so stunned that I couldn't even process what was happening, much less asking about the next steps. They don't even know if he'll remain conscious. I think it's still touch and go."

Jessica hadn't said a word since being at the hospital, but could no longer contain her panic.

"What if he stays alive? Awake? Who's gonna take care of him? Felicia, I know you don't want him here, and he's gonna need 24 hour care. You and Mitchell are trying to..."

Carolyn cut her off.

"Jessica! Stop! He may not even stay awake. Hell, he could drift back into a coma and die before nightfall." Everyone heard the wishful thinking in Carolyn's voice, but no one commented. "The bottom line is we really don't know anything, at least not enough to start making plans and arrangements."

Felicia was wrapped in Mitchell's arms, but looked up at Carolyn as she spoke.

"Carolyn, I really appreciated having you guys around. You guys have been really good to me – to us, but I wouldn't expect you to stick around for whatever's next. You guys served your time with him."

Carolyn responded, representing Jessica as well.

"Look, if you told me a few months ago that I would EVER be sitting in Kenneth's living room having a conversation with his wife, I would've told you that you were insane. But here we are. I'm cold but I'm not cold enough to walk away and leave you knee-deep in this mess. That's right, Number 3, we're not gonna abandon you now."

Carolyn saw the tears welling in Felicia's eyes, which was her cue to kill the moment.

"Now, don't get me wrong - I'm sure I'm not finished giving you hell yet. You're way too uptight, and you let that crazy ass man jack with your self-esteem. And if Mitchell plans to stick around, I'm gonna need you to lay down the law, cuz we're not taking any more crap from any more men!"

Felicia and Mitchell looked at each other and smiled, while Carolyn continued with a more solemn tone. "Man, just when we thought we'd made peace with everything, Kenneth comes back from the dead. But I'll tell you what — if he pulls through this, he's gonna wish his ass was dead! He was such a bad ass with each of us individually, let's see how tough he is with ALL of us together!"

Each lady chuckled enjoying Carolyn's proclamation. Mitchell smiled but chose to stay out of it.

Carolyn raised her glass. "I don't know what the future holds, but tonight, we drink!"

TWO

It had been a week since Kenneth opened his eyes, but Felicia still hadn't been back to the hospital. She couldn't face him until she understood what she was feeling. She spent months hoping and praying he'd come back to her, but after discovering who he really was, it took only weeks for her to realize she could, and wanted to live without him. Though she'd never admit it to anyone, she was afraid she'd fall back into a place of intimidation. Rational or not, she knew her feelings were real.

Mitchell watched Felicia as she struggled through the emotions, and though she tried to downplay the stress, Mitchell knew she needed his unconditional support. So he stayed at her house...in the guestroom. Night after night, he dreamed of holding Felicia in his arms, but knew he couldn't...not like that...not yet. Each night, he slept in a bed less than 30 feet and a closed door from his future.

Kenneth was on Mitchell's mind almost as much as he was on Felicia's. His conscience wouldn't allow him to wish death on any man, but based on how Kenneth treated Felicia and the other ladies, he certainly didn't wish him well. Mitchell avoided asking Felicia her thoughts on caring for Kenneth, but felt strongly that Kenneth deserved no compassion, and definitely no effort from Felicia. Regardless of his opinion, Kenneth and Felicia were still married, they had a new baby together, and Mitchell would have to just ride it out.

On a cool, rainy morning, Felicia awoke with nothing but the hospital on her mind. She pulled herself together, dropped Emmanuel off at the sitter, and mustered up the strength to go to the hospital. As she sat in the parking lot with the engine running, she leaned back and closed her eyes. She wanted to pray but quickly realized she didn't know what to pray for. Felicia knew it was wrong to pray for Kenneth's demise, but she also knew she had no desire to go back to a life that included him. So, she prayed for the strength to do the right thing, whatever that looked like. With a big, deep breath, she turned off the car and opened the door.

Felicia was in such deep thought that she had no idea how she got from the car to Kenneth's floor. There she stood, near the elevator, staring down the long, white hallway. She could feel her heart racing, as her breath became more and more shallow. She knew she had to move, so Felicia pushed herself forward and began to walk.

Standing in the room doorway, Felicia felt as if she were on a diving board. She took a deep breath, and stepped forward. There he was, lying slightly inclined and staring out the large window. Felicia's purse hit the room door, startling Kenneth. Slowly, he turned. His eyes lit up, using muscles that had been dormant for months. Kenneth worked to push the button on the bed's controller, while struggling to adjust his body.

As Felicia walked slowly toward the bed, she absorbed Kenneth's appearance. The cotton hospital gown looked 3 sizes too big, loose around the neck and arms. His face was drawn and aged. This once big, loud, intimidating man now looked so frail, so weak. She thought her first emotion would be resentment, but instead, it was pity. She spoke softly.

"Hi Stranger, welcome back."

As Felicia smiled slightly, she moved directly to the chair. She quickly realized he was watching her every move, so she dropped her purse in the seat and walked to the opposite side of the bed. Felicia leaned over the bed toward him, and

Kenneth closed his eyes in anticipation of her warmth and affection. Instead, he received a soft tug of his overgrown beard and a peck on the forehead. Before she could pull away, Felicia felt Kenneth's trembling hand on her arm and his head attempting to nuzzle into the nape of her neck. She felt conflicted. His touch triggered forgotten feelings, while her mind reflected on the months of painful discoveries. She pulled away, but not before she pasted on a smile.

"How do you feel?"

It wasn't until Felicia settled in her seat that she realized Kenneth hadn't responded. She looked up, and there he sat, staring at her like a lost little boy. Then it hit her – Kenneth couldn't speak. Felicia tried to downplay her surprise.

"Well, you look a lot better than I expected. Sorry I haven't been here. As you can see by my flattened belly, there's someone at home keeping me busy."

Kenneth tried to smile as Felicia continued.

"His name is Emmanuel, and he's amazing. Here's a picture of him. Wait, can you focus?"

Kenneth slowly shook his head yes. Felicia frantically scrolled through the pictures on her phone until she came to one of Emmanuel's more expressive shots. She leaned forward and held the phone close to Kenneth's face. Kenneth squinted, then smiled wide enough for his teeth to peek out from between his chapped lips. Felicia had no idea she was smiling as well.

"Yep, that's him. When you're feeling better, I'll bring him to see you."

Crap. What had she committed to? Within only a few minutes of being around Kenneth, Felicia realized she was already making promises to please him. She could feel herself heading down a path of nervous chatter, so Felicia began her escape by rising and quickly pulling her purse into the bend of her arm. Just as she was about to explain her need for a sudden departure, she heard her name from behind her. It was Dr. Walsh.

"Felicia? Hi, can I speak with you for a minute?"

Thank goodness, Felicia thought.

"Get some rest. I'll be back soon."

Felicia could feel Kenneth's expression changing, but refused to acknowledge it. She couldn't allow herself to be pulled in.

As she turned into the hall, she saw Dr. Walsh standing there, looking a bit frustrated. He leaned in toward her, as if to ensure he wasn't overheard. "Felicia, where have you been? Kenneth's been awake for over a week. Is there something wrong with the baby?"

Felicia knew Dr. Walsh's concern was genuine, so she took no offense to his inquiry. "No, the baby's fine. This has just been a bit overwhelming for me." Felicia hung her head. "I was planning to come sooner, but...well, I just couldn't."

Dr. Walsh took a deep breath, but kept his voice low. "Look, Felicia, I certainly don't want to overstep, but this is a really crucial time for Kenneth. His recovery could be based on how strong he is emotionally. He needs to know he has you in his corner. He needs to know your love for him hasn't changed."

Oh, but it had. Felicia didn't dare share what she knew with Dr. Walsh, so she just smiled and shook her head. She knew continuing the conversation would only make her feel guilty, so it was time to make her escape.

"I'll be back soon – just call me if you need me. Thanks, Doctor."

Felicia visited the hospital a few more times in the next week. Though he still couldn't speak, Felicia could see progress in his mobility, and energy level. The doctor said the day after he awoke, he could hardly keep his eyes opened, but now, just weeks after his miraculous return, Kenneth was sitting up, and lifting his arms. Most of the hospital staff was impressed and elated that they witnessed such a great recovery, except Paige, the nurse who cared for him while Felicia learned of his many demons. Paige was professional, but completely disinterested in anything more than the bare minimum for Kenneth.

Though she knew it was the right thing to do, Felicia struggled with her treks to the hospital. It was hard to watch Kenneth improve and not rattle off a barrage of questions. And though she could never admit it to anyone, she struggled with how involved to be with his recovery. Her nature was to nurture. Her instinct was to take care of anyone who needed her, but each time she walked down the cold hospital hall, all she wanted to do was go home. This time, as Felicia made her way to see Kenneth, the nurse's annoyed voice broke her dismal train of thought.

As she crossed the threshold, she saw Marie standing near Kenneth's bed, waving her finger at the patient.

"Mr. Wilson, I need you to cooperate. I know you don't want me to call Paige, the floor supervisor! You've been in bed for months, and you've got to start using those muscles again. Now come on, please try to stand up."

Felicia's greeting sounded more protective than she planned.

"What's going on? Kenneth, are you giving Miss Marie a hard time?"

Marie spun around startled, then relieved.

"Oh, Mrs. Wilson, thank goodness! The doctor has instructed us to get Mr. Wilson up and moving a little each day, but he doesn't want to cooperate. Maybe he'll listen to you." Marie turned back toward Kenneth. "Mr. Wilson, don't you want to get out of here and home to your beautiful family? You can't do that if you don't get better."

Felicia was fine with Marie's pep talk, until she mentioned Kenneth coming home. Felicia stepped between Marie and Kenneth's bed, and leaned in toward him.

"Kenneth, what are you doing? Why won't you just do what the nurses are asking? I know being here and taking orders is driving you crazy, but it's the only way you're going to get better and be released. Why won't you just cooperate?"

Kenneth hung his head like a scolded child as Felicia continued.

"Come on, these ladies don't have time for your antics, and frankly, neither do I. Now, swing your legs around here and try to stand up. We will spot you, but you have to at least try."

Felicia spoke to Kenneth like never before, but she wasn't sure if he even noticed. He just stared down at his cracked fingernails and dry hands. Then it hit her. Kenneth wasn't used to looking this way. He was weak. He was homely. He was ashamed. For a moment, Felicia felt sorry for him, but quickly realized she now had a bargaining chip. Felicia pulled the chair up to the side of the bed and leaned in as closely as possible.

"Listen, I know what's wrong. Here's the deal – you swing your legs around and try to stand up just once, and I'll have you groomed and cleaned up, just the way you like. Deal?"

Kenneth's head didn't move but he raised his eyes to meet Felicia's. He slowly raised his right hand and pointed at Felicia. She knew what he wanted.

"Fine, I'll groom you. Now start moving."

Marie had become engulfed in the local news broadcast while Felicia was making deals, but scampered to his side when she realized he was trying to move. Together the two ladies balanced and braced Kenneth, while he slowly slid off the bed to his unsteady feet and trembling legs. After a few seconds , Kenneth leaned back on the bed, winded and surprised. Marie squealed with excitement.

"You did it! See, I knew you could!"

Kenneth looked over at Felicia for her approval, but all she could give him was a polite smile as she reached for her purse.

"Good job. I'll bring your grooming kit when I come back. See you soon."

Days passed since Felicia made her deal with Kenneth, but she knew as Mitchell prepped for work, today was the day she'd hold up her end. Though Mitchell inquired about Kenneth's progress, Felicia chose not to mention the agreement to groom him. She considered it on occasion, but couldn't come up with a the right words. Everything she considered saying made her sound too involved with his recovery.

Once Mitchell pulled out of the driveway, Felicia headed to the Master closet and recovered Kenneth's grooming kit. It was impressive - full of tools, creams and aftershaves. Kenneth said he believed in having his own kit and taking his tools to the shops with him, but based on recent discoveries, she had no idea who had been grooming him. The aroma in the soft leather bag triggered memories, and Felicia felt her mind drifting back to a happier time. Before things got out of hand, she dropped the bag on the bed, and hopped in the shower.

Felicia arrived at the hospital just in time to see Kenneth attempting to feed himself. He was slow and methodical, but still had tremors, so the majority of his meal rested safely on his chest. Felicia stood in the doorway and watched. Seeing Kenneth vulnerable was rare, so she used the moment to gain enough compassion to get her through the task at hand.

"Well, it's a good thing I came today. At this rate, you'd starve."

Kenneth turned toward the door, startled. He lost his concentration and dropped the fork, but didn't care. He was just happy to see Felicia.

"Are you finished eating? Do you want more?" Felicia asked as she unpacked her goods. Kenneth shook his head no as he pushed the rolling table away. Kenneth was eager to be touched by his wife.

"Okay, grooming it is." As Felicia cleared the table and looked around the room for an outlet, she could feel Kenneth watching her every move. She found a reality show on TV and turned up the volume. "Here's something for you to focus on while I work. Let's start with this beard."

Time flew and before Felicia knew it, she had been at the hospital for hours. She gave Kenneth a clean shave and facial, cut and edged his hair, and ended his day with a manicure and pedicure. She even splashed a little after shave on his face, which he enjoyed immensely. Kenneth's inability to speak and Felicia's desire to do a good job allowed them both to relax and enjoy the day.

Felicia packed up the kit, while Kenneth lay perfectly still, smiling. When Felicia realized she was being watched, she stopped and smiled. With a gentle pat on the shoulder, Felicia whispered, "Much better." As she tried to walk away, Kenneth grabbed Felicia's hand and rested his face in her palm. He closed his eyes and took deep breaths. Felicia stood still until she heard Marie's voice in the hall. She pulled away from Kenneth, snatched her purse from the chair, and hit the door just as Marie walked in to admire Kenneth's new look.

Felicia hadn't planned to spend all day at the hospital, but did. Though she still had errands to run, she was determined to beat Mitchell home. She was taking Emmanuel's jacket off when she heard Mitchell's key tickle the lock.

"Hey Babe, how was your day?"

Mitchell made a beeline to Felicia, but his kiss was blocked by Emmanuel's happy hands and feet. Once Mitchell took hold of Emmanuel, he leaned in for his kiss. Felicia gently stroked his cheek. Mitchell stopped mid-kiss, and tilted his face toward her hand.

"What's that?"

"What's what?"

"Your hand – it smells like men's cologne."

Felicia stalled by taking Emmanuel back and walking toward the kitchen. "Oh, that. The nurses wanted Kenneth's grooming kit, and I spilled his after shave. I just got home and haven't had a chance to wash it off yet."

Felicia's uncomfortable response made Mitchell a little suspicious, but he decided to leave it alone for the moment.

After Kenneth's grooming appointment, Felicia began to visit the hospital without dread. Felicia's daily arrival always sparked enthusiasm in Kenneth. His eyes would light up, and he worked harder on moving and mouthing more words. Felicia always let the nurses and therapists take the lead, but by the time the visit was over, she was encouraging him and managing his day. Kenneth made it easy. He wasn't the same control freak she knew before the accident. He was engaged, hopeful, and appreciative. He had no idea what Felicia discovered during his long slumber.

Days turned into weeks, and Kenneth's progress allowed him to be moved onto a different floor before his eventual move to a rehabilitation facility. As Felicia headed toward his new room, she was met at the corner by Dr. Walsh.

"Felicia, how are you?"

"I'm hanging in there. I had plans to reach out to you this week. How is your patient progressing?"

Dr. Walsh dropped his hands in his pockets. "He's doing quite well, especially for someone who's been out as long as he has. His vitals remain stable, and his strength is increasing. We're going to continue running tests on his brain function, but so far, we aren't seeing anything that would keep him from having a long, productive life."

Dr. Walsh smiled as he shared the good news, but Felicia could only smirk and give a slight head nod.

"That's great news, Doc. So, what are the next steps?"

"Well, once we feel comfortable that he won't relapse, we'll need to move him, then – "

Felicia interrupted. "Move him? Move him where? I mean, where is he supposed to go? Surely I'm not expected to take care of him and the baby. I'm just getting used to..."

Dr. Walsh was caught off guard by Felicia's response. "Felicia, relax. He's a long way from being able to go home. He'll need to be moved into a rehabilitation facility first. He'll have round the clock care, nutrition, and physical therapy. It could be months before he's ready to come home. That should give you plenty of time to prepare for his arrival, and I'm guessing, a big celebration."

Felicia again smiled and hung her head, thinking about his homecoming and first conversation. "Yes, extra time is good."

Dr. Walsh looked at his watch. "Ok, well, I'm off to see a few more patients, so I'll leave you to your visit. See you soon."

"Thanks Doc." Felicia took a deep breath and turned into Kenneth's room. Dr. Walsh triggered renewed anxiety in Felicia. Felicia had just gotten used to seeing Kenneth alert and functioning, but she wasn't ready to think about him being back out into the world – her world.

Kenneth's new digs were quite different than his last. His new room had pastel blue walls and floral linens. The room felt more healing than sterile. The nurses said that newly conscious patients respond positively to color. His window faced the lush hills and forest behind the hospital, which made for a beautiful sunset on clear days.

Kenneth was facing the door when Felicia turned into the room. He immediately began to prop himself up as if to display his progress since their last visit. Felicia smiled but chose to distract herself with anything she could. Her mind was still on Dr. Walsh's words.

"Hey there. It looks like you got plenty of rest yesterday. I just saw Dr. Walsh and he said you're making decent progress."

Felicia didn't want to sound eager for his recovery, so she quickly countered her comment.

"No rush, though. After all, you've got a lot of work ahead of you. Looks like you need more water. I'll just grab your pitcher and be right back."

Before Felicia could grab the pale pink pitcher and escape, she heard a faint, breathy word.

"Fe..li..cia. Hi...Fe..li..cia..."

Felicia froze in her tracks. A chill raced down her spine. She didn't realize she dropped the half full plastic pitcher. Water splattered everywhere and the pitcher bounced around on the tile while the top rolled out of the room and down the hall. Kenneth had been mouthing words and relying on facial expressions to communicate, but nothing had been as clear as her name.

Felicia slowly turned to face Kenneth.

"What did you say?"

"Hi...Fe...li...cia..."

Felicia knew she couldn't hide her shock, so she smiled uncomfortably and left.

THREE

After the shock of hearing Kenneth's voice, Felicia chose to stay away from the hospital for a few days. Hearing Kenneth speak her name confused Felicia. She knew he was relying solely on her, and in a strange way, she liked it. She told herself she loved being in control of a man who used to control her, but the reality was that she enjoyed seeing the progress he was making first hand. Somehow when Felicia was with him, she was able to disconnect from the chaos that was to come. She took notes at physical therapy, and even participated in some of the exercises. The more time Felicia spent with Kenneth, the more determined Kenneth was to get well. As far as he was concerned, he had a family to get back to. Her days at the hospital were getting longer and longer, and Mitchell found himself spending more time with Emmanuel, and less time with Felicia.

Portland hadn't seen sunshine for days, so the sound of chirping birds first thing in the morning was a welcome surprise. Felicia was exhausted, but awoke willingly when she felt soft kisses in the nape of her neck. Mitchell was up, dressed, and ready to hit the road.

"Good Morning, Lovely."

Felicia slowly rolled over to face her greeter. "Mmmm, Good Morning, and I'm sure I'm not lovely. I just hope I don't look as tired as I feel."

Mitchell leaned against the headboard and pulled Felicia up and onto his chest. "You're as beautiful as you were the day I saw you arguing in that restaurant, but I know the hospital visits are draining you. I've gotta hand it to you. I don't know how you're able to even be around him, much less pretend to want him to get well."

Felicia knew Mitchell meant no harm, but she still felt compelled to respond. "I need to be there, Mitch. The doctor said he needs support as he's going through this. No matter how I feel about him, he's still Emmanuel's father."

They hadn't really discussed Kenneth's recovery since he opened his eyes, but Mitchell certainly wasn't expecting Felicia to be so defensive. "It's fine Felicia, really. I'm not saying you shouldn't be there. I'm just saying you're handling it well, that's all. Look, we obviously need some time together. Why don't we get Carolyn to watch Emmanuel tonight, and let's get out of the house. We can go to dinner and maybe a movie. I want to spend some time with you – just you and me."

Felicia pulled up enough to give Mitchell a quick peck before climbing out of bed. "Sounds good, Babe. You make the plans. I've got to catch up on errands today, but I'll be back long before you get home."

Mitchell hopped off the bed. "Great – I will see you, say, 6ish?"

"6ish it is!" Felicia glanced back with a coy smile as she flipped her robe over her shoulder and scooted to the bathroom.

She hadn't mentioned it to Mitchell, but Felicia decided this was the day she'd confront Kenneth about his past. Though she played the potential conversation over and over in her head, but could only see her side of it. How would he react? Would he be remorseful and apologetic, or arrogant and mean? Surely he wouldn't be cocky, especially in his current state.

Felicia took care of her errands before heading to the hospital, since she didn't know what the visit would hold. When she arrived, Kenneth was receiving assistance with his lunch from Marie. His eyes twinkled every when he saw Felicia in the doorway.

"Hey you." Felicia said. The greeting was the same but her tone was quite different.

"Hi." Kenneth mumbled as he tried to swallow a mouth full of mashed potatoes.

"Hello, Mrs. Wilson, chirped Marie. Kenneth is finally getting his appetite back. We've been working on his motor skills, but today, he was too hungry to be patient. Would you like to take over for me?"

Felicia countered before Marie could complete the question.

"Oh, no, no thank you. You're doing just fine."

Felicia's abrupt response warranted a confused look from both Kenneth and Marie.

After a few more bites, Kenneth was ready to talk with his wife. "No more," he whispered.

"Are you sure?" Marie asked.

"No more." Kenneth still spoke with a whisper, but frowned to let her know he was certain.

"Okay, I'll give you lovebirds some privacy." Marie smiled as she lifted the tray from the table and headed for the door.

Kenneth struggled as he turned toward Felicia. Over the weeks she'd seen significant progress in his recovery, but things such as shifting his weight were still difficult. Felicia dreaded this conversation, but knew she had to at least get the ball rolling. She made her way to the perfectly positioned chair at Kenneth's bedside.

"Kenneth, I need to discuss some things with you." Kenneth's expression changed from bliss to concern, which made Felicia even more uncomfortable. She decided to ease into it.

"Do you remember anything about your accident?"

Kenneth looked down at the TV remote resting in his lap. He spoke slowly and methodically, but his volume was still very low, so Felicia leaned in a bit.

"I was on my way home. It was raining." He paused. "I don't…I don't know any more than that. I don't remember. Fe-li-cia…I just don't remember."

Felicia continued her inquiry. "Do you remember other things? You know, like, your past? Your marriages, or say, your normal life routine?"

Kenneth squinted as he concentrated. "I don't know. Some. I don't know…just don't know!"

Felicia could see Kenneth's eyes beginning to water as he realized chunks of his past were missing and instinctively responded with compassion. "It's okay, Kenneth. It's okay. I'm sure it will all come back to you. It's just going to take some time."

Kenneth turned away from Felicia as one tear escaped. "I'm tired, Fe-li-cia..." Kenneth pushed the bed remote and reclined slowly. Felicia slowly rose from her seat.

"You get some rest. I know you have your assessment this afternoon. I'll be back later, okay?

"Okay." Kenneth mumbled, but never looked back.

Felicia left the facility but had no desire to go home. Kenneth's memory issues presented a completely different set of problems. It began to sprinkle, so she went to a local mall and sat in the atrium. Felicia appeared to be people watching, but didn't see a single face. Her thoughts were a million miles away. What if he didn't remember anything about his past? If he didn't remember, how could she confront him about it? She'd be yelling at a man who had absolutely no idea what she was talking about. The lies, abuse, adultery, and criminal activity would all be news to him. Would he expect her to stay with him, since he didn't remember? What if she stayed and his memory came back? Felicia's head was spinning. She walked around the mall for a while, still in a daze. Before she knew it, it was time to go back to the hospital for Kenneth's assessment.

Mitchell paced, then sat as he tried not to call Felicia's unanswered phone for the third time. "What time did you tell her to be here?" Carolyn looked up from the floor palette where she and Emmanuel played.

"We said 6ish, but she said she had a lot of errands to run since she's been spending so much time at the hospital."

Carolyn leaned forward.

"Yeah, what's up with that? I get that she's got to be there on occasion, to sign paperwork and such, but why is she spending so much time there?"

Mitchell sat up from his seat and leaned toward Carolyn. "I don't know. Carolyn, this is a bizarre situation. I mean, I'm spending the majority of my time here, helping around the house and with the baby, but Felicia is hardly around. Don't get me wrong, there is no place I'd rather be, and I get that she needs to spend time with Kenneth, but, well...I don't know. I can't tell what she's thinking, and she's not talking about it. I gave her a compliment today and she nearly bit my head off."

Carolyn needed Mitchell to say what she was thinking. "You don't know what? Why she's with him so much, especially after finding out who he really is?"

Mitchell felt better letting Carolyn say the words. "Well, yeah, sorta. I mean, I didn't expect her to cut him off completely, or leave him stranded in that hospital, but I guess I didn't expect her to be there as much as she is. I was kind of hoping we'd be, you know, moving forward by now."

"Moving forward where, in bed?" Carolyn threw herself backward, cackling and slapping her knee. Emmanuel found her gestures hilarious, and began banging the giant Legos on the floor while laughing hysterically, as if he understood Carolyn's wit.

Mitchell quickly countered. "Shut up, Carolyn. No that's not it. Well, that's not all of it. I knew when he woke up, our plans would change and things be different, but I guess I wasn't expecting them to be this different." Mitchell looked at his watch for the third time during the conversation, then popped up and snatched his tucked dress shirt out of his pants. "Okay, well, it's almost 9. You might as well go on home. I'll order a pizza or something when she gets here."

Just as Carolyn began to pull herself up with the help of the ottoman, they heard the key in the door. The apologies began before they saw a face.

"I am so sorry Babe, I got sidetracked, and the cleaners couldn't find my blue jacket, I almost ran out of gas because I forgot to fill up the truck yesterday, and well, there was a lot more going on at Kenneth's physical therapy than I realized."

Mitchell met Felicia with a kiss as she entered the room. "Hey, look, don't worry about it. It was just dinner and a movie. So, I didn't realize you were going to the hospital. I guess I thought you were just running errands today."

Felicia explained while scooping up and snuggling Emmanuel. "Well, I wasn't planning on it, but I had to do some things in that area so I just popped in. When I got there, they were doing an assessment to decide how close he is to be being released."

"Released?" Mitchell and Carolyn responded in harmony, but Carolyn took the ball and ran with it. "Released? And where the hell do they expect him to go? Why are you involved in that? I know you're not planning to bring his sorry ass back here, are you?"

Felicia adjusted Emmanuel on her hip as she turned toward Carolyn. "No, Carolyn, he's got to go to a rehab facility first. He still can't do a lot of things. They want me involved because I'm still his wife...at least on paper." Felicia felt compelled to look over at Mitchell as she ended the sentence. "Besides, he doesn't remember anything."

Both Carolyn and Mitchell leaned forward as Felicia sat and pulled her shoes off.

Mitchell spoke up. "What do you mean? How do you know he doesn't remember anything?" Mitchell tried to play it cool, but was dying to hear her response.

"Well, the doctor told me that because there was some head trauma, he could have some memory issues, both long and short term," Felicia smiled and bounced Emmanuel on her knee so she didn't have to make eye contact with anyone else. "I've been feeling him out, even asked him about the accident. All he remembered was driving in the rain."

"Bullshit!" Carolyn shouted.

"Carolyn!" Felicia barked.

"No – bullshit! He remembers every second of his sorry ass life! He just doesn't want to admit it, because now he needs help. Felicia, don't forget who we're dealing with. He's a professional liar! He knows he's in a bind – he just doesn't know how much you know!"

Mitchell was thinking the same thing, but was happy it came from Carolyn.

"Carolyn, I know who we're dealing with. I'm not just going by what he's saying. The doctors are able to see the brain damage on his MRIs. The damage is real. I haven't forgotten anything, I assure you. He's going to face the music, I promise you."

"Okay, just don't get pulled back into his shit, Felicia. He may look weak and helpless, but he's still the same person. He's still the devil."

"I know, Carolyn."

It was obvious Felicia didn't want to continue the conversation, so Carolyn kissed the baby, grabbed her jacket, and gave Mitchell a supportive nod before heading to the door.

Felicia reached for Mitchell's hand and pulled him over to the couch. She barely waited for him to sit before she scooted as close to him as possible. Emmanuel immediately began crawling from lap to lap happily. Mitchell felt Carolyn provided the perfect opening, so he took it. "So, Babe, how long will Kenneth be in the rehab facility?"

Felicia's tone changed slightly. "I don't know. It could be a few months, or it could be only one. It depends on how well he does, and how fast he does it."

"So, have you given any thought to what you want to do after that?"

Felicia looked up. "What do you mean?"

"I mean, when are you going to tell him what you know? I get that you want to wait until he's doing better, but you don't want to make him think he's coming back to you, do you?"

Felicia pivoted to face Mitchell, while Emmanuel stood in his lap, sticking his fingers in Mitchell's mouth and humming happily.

"I don't know when I'm going to tell him, Mitch. You know, this situation isn't easy. I'm trying to do the right thing. Do you think I want to be there with him? Do you think I want to be his cheerleader? He can hardly speak, so we don't know how much of his life he even remembers. Right now, my focus is to get him over to the rehab facility, find out if he's competent, and do what I need to do to get on with my life."

Mitchell knew he had to choose his words and tone carefully. "I understand - I do. And I'm gonna support you in any way I can. I guess I'm just eager to get on with our lives."

Felicia's expression softened. "I know Honey. I am too. But I want to make sure we do this the right way, so it can't come back to haunt us, you know?"

"Yeah, I know."

"Good. Now, I'm going to put this little man to bed, and maybe we can have some Chinese food delivered and catch some mindless TV?"

Mitchell felt better. "Sounds like a plan. But promise me we'll keep talking through this stuff, okay?"

Felicia moved Emmanuel fingers and gave Mitchell a quick peck. "Okay, I promise. Get the menus."

FOUR

"Ok, Mr. Wilson, are you ready to head over to your new digs?"
Marie made the rehab facility sound interesting and exciting.

"Yes," Kenneth responded softly. "I am."

"Good! Now, I've told them they better take good care of you,
or they'll have to deal with me!" Marie smiled and winked
while helping navigate the gurney into the ambulance.

Felicia poked her head in behind Marie. "Kenneth, I'll meet
you over there." Kenneth smiled and nodded as they closed
the doors.

As she drove, Felicia's mind raced. A few weeks ago, Mitchell
brought up some very important issues, and though she

promised to discuss her concerns, they hadn't talked about Kenneth since their derailed date night. What would the next few months look like? Would Kenneth be able to make it on his own, or would he need assistance for the rest of his life? Would she be responsible for him? And at what point would he ready to talk about this other life he led? The moment her mind drifted to her discoveries, Felicia's compassion disappeared. But she knew the only way to manage her emotions was to get on top of his long term arrangements.

Felicia stayed in the rehab facility just long enough to get a quick tour, sign paperwork, and ensure Kenneth was settled. She asked a few questions about his schedule, and was off.

As the days progressed, things became more hectic. Emmanuel was irritable and teething, the house was a mess, Mitchell was working longer hours, and the rehab facility asked that Felicia become more involved with the Kenneth's recovery.

Felicia finally had a day to catch up, so with the first sign of dawn, she hit the ground running. She cleaned, did laundry, and even caught up on some paperwork before Emmanuel woke up. Felicia decided to take advantage of the quiet and shower steam for a few extra minutes. It felt wonderful. Just as she stepped out of the shower the phone rang. Felicia flung the towel around her and stumbled into the bedroom. It was Dr. Walsh.

"Hi Felicia – Dr. Walsh here. Sorry to disturb you, but I'd like to make a suggestion in the interest of Kenneth's recovery."

This should be good, Felicia thought. "Yes Doctor, what is it?"

"I think it's time for Kenneth to meet his son. His recovery is coming along, but I really think he's at a crossroads, and needs a bit of a spark. Seeing his boy for the first time could be exactly what he needs. Of course, it's your call, but I really think it could help."

Felicia didn't have the energy to share her thoughts on Kenneth's parental rights. She needed to talk with Dr. Walsh in person about the impact a divorce could have anyway, so she thanked him for his time, and told him they'd discuss it and more in person. Just as she turned to back toward the bathroom, the phone rang again. It was Mitchell.

"Hey it's me. How are you feeling?"

Felicia wanted to stay on task.

"Hi Honey – look, I'm in a hurry. Can I call you later?"

"Yes you can, but what's going on?"

"I'm heading to the rehab facility. The doctor said he needs to talk to me."

"Any idea what's going on?"

Felicia felt the need to avoid yet another conversation. "No, not really. I'm guessing it's about Kenneth's progress."

"Felicia, have you given any more thought to when you're going to talk to Kenneth? I'm worried that-"

The combination of Mitchell's inquiries and Emmanuel's screaming quickly sent Felicia to her tipping point.

"Mitch, I'm gonna tell him, ok? Please, just let me manage the timing. You know you don't have anything to worry about. There obviously is nothing going on with Kenneth and me. He just got out of a coma, for Pete's sake! What do you think I'm over there doing, holding his hand and talking about old times? Sitting on his lap in the wheelchair? I'm simply there to..."

"Felicia – Felicia, stop!" Mitchell's concerned turned to irritation. "I was about to say, I'm concerned you're not taking care of yourself. Of course I don't think anything is going on between you two, and I understand your responsibility in this. I just want you to be okay."

Felicia felt stupid and embarrassed. "I'm sorry and you're right. I'm just tired I guess, which proves your point. As soon as the doctor gives me the green light, I'm going to tell him we're done." Mitchell knew he remained stuck in a 'wait and see' mode, but didn't push his luck. "Okay. Go do your thing. I'll talk with you later."

Felicia exhaled as she hung up. She didn't dare tell Mitchell that she was taking Emmanuel to see Kenneth. She was telling herself that her plan was for Emmanuel to miraculously heal Kenneth so they could go their separate ways.

As the automatic doors opened at the facility, the nurses lit up. Felicia barely got through the door before Jennifer, the head nurse was in front of her and reaching for Emmanuel. "Well Hello, Little Prince! You are adorable!" Emmanuel was always willing to spend time with a happy lady, and immediately extended his arms.

"Oh Felicia, the pictures don't do him justice! He's beautiful."

Felicia never got tired of hearing that. "Thank you Jennifer. He's a little irritable today – teething."

"Oh, I can't imagine this sweet baby irritable." Come on, Kenneth is in the physical therapy room." Jennifer escorted Felicia to the room while cooing and playing with Emmanuel. Emmanuel was more interested in where they were going than who he was with.

Felicia entered the room first. Kenneth was in the corner with the therapist, doing repetitions of standing and sitting. He turned toward the door to see Felicia standing there, expressionless. Did this mean Kenneth would be walking soon? Felicia stepped aside slightly, just enough for Jennifer to move up beside her. Kenneth's jaw dropped as he slowly lowered himself back into the chair.

"My son," he said, though the words were more breath than volume. "Give me my son."

Jennifer chuckled as she walked toward him. "Okay, okay! You get yourself situated in that chair first. I know you think you're fine, but I'm not sitting this baby in your lap until I'm sure you're steady."

The therapist helped Kenneth adjust himself until he appeared to be settled. Jennifer slowly lowered Emmanuel into Kenneth's lap. Emmanuel complied, but kept a grip on the sleeve of Jennifer's scrubs. Felicia moved in closely to supervise the handoff. Jennifer gently released Emmanuel's hand.

"It's okay, Baby. He's you're daddy." Emmanuel looked up at his mother, then slowly around to Kenneth. Kenneth smiled as best he could, but inside, he was beaming.

"Hi Little Man," Kenneth whispered. Emmanuel turned toward Felicia and his look of wonder quickly changed to misery. He whined while his face contorted into sheer horror, and he let out a wail, reaching for his mommy. Felicia dove in to retrieve him before he could disturb the whole facility.

"He's teething, so he's not in the best of moods. Come here Baby, it's okay." Emmanuel quickly calmed down once he was back in Felicia's arms. Tears welled in Kenneth's eyes as he sat in awe.

"He's perfect."

Felicia was startled by a hand on her shoulder. It was Dr. Herman, Kenneth's new physician. Felicia met him during the transfer, but assumed Dr. Walsh would remain involved as well.

"Hello Felicia. And who is this handsome young man?" The doctor bent forward to get eye to eye with Emmanuel. Emmanuel was no longer in the mood to socialize and quickly nuzzled his face into Felicia's neck.

"This is Emmanuel. Can we walk and talk, Doctor?" Felicia glanced back at Kenneth. "We'll be back." Kenneth smiled and nodded but knew that was probably the end of today's visit.

"Felicia, Kenneth is doing well. I carefully review every case before I take them over, and rest assured, you don't have anything to worry about. He has the potential to make a full recovery."

Felicia didn't know how to feel about the news. "That's good. Doctor, Kenneth and I have some pretty serious issues we've got to talk through. When can I begin having those conversations? I don't want to impact his recovery, but time is of the essence, and his long term plans could be impacted."

The doctor's expression changed to concern. "Uh, well I don't know. I mean, you never know what can impact a person's recovery. I can tell you that Kenneth is working as hard as he can to get back home to his family. Will your conversations impact his motivation?

Felicia dropped her head. "Yes, probably. While he was in the coma, some things came out, and well, he won't be coming back home. He and I won't be together."

Dr. Herman stopped walking. "Felicia, you can't tell him that – it could derail his whole recovery. You've got to give him some time to get himself together. Have you given any thought to where he will go? Is there someone that could take care of him?"

"I don't know. I mean, I haven't gotten that far. All I know is he can't come back home."

Dr. Herman could tell this was a situation he didn't want to get mixed up in, so he treaded lightly. "Felicia, whatever happened between you and Kenneth is none of my business, and you have to do what you have to do. But just know his recovery relies on his emotional well-being as much as it does his physical health."

"I understand. How long before he'll be ready to leave here?" Emmanuel had dozed off and was now dead weight, so Felicia had to shift hips while she exhaled her question.

"If things continue to go well, he could be released in about a month. You need to start making arrangements now. He'll still need physical therapy and some help at home, or, wherever he is."

"Thanks, Doctor." Felicia had no desire to return to the room. "Will you please tell him I had to run?" Before Dr. Herman could respond, Felicia turned and was heading toward the door. She gave a slight smile as the she passed the cooing ladies at the reception desk.

Emmanuel was sleeping well, so Felicia decided she'd postpone her other errands and get him home. She strategically removed him from the car seat, and walked gingerly through the house to the nursery. Just as she released him to the comfort of his crib, the doorbell rang. Emmanuel flinched, but didn't open his eyes. Felicia had no idea who would be showing up at this time of day, unannounced.

Felicia looked through the peephole to see a well-dressed man. She cautiously cracked the door, and discovered that there were actually two men. One was very tall, broad shoulders and bald. The other was just a bit taller than Felicia. At first glance, the short one looked like a kindly grandfather. He had wavy white hair and brown eyes. His face looked a bit weathered, but his well-groomed beard and tailored suit made it clear that his tan was a result of leisure, not hard work. His open shirt collar without a tie was probably as casual as he ever dressed.

"Yes? Can I help you?"

The large man spoke as he attempted to look past Felicia and through the house. "Mrs. Wilson?"

"What can I do for you?"

"Is your husband around?"

"No. What can I do for you?"

"My name is Johnathon Napoli. This is my uncle, Carmine. We're associates of your husband. May we come in?"

Felicia scoffed, "Uh, no. Again gentlemen, what can I do for you?"

Johnathon looked down at his uncle, who appeared to be impressed with Felicia's climbing roses, so he continued. "Mrs. Wilson, I assure you, it will only take a minute. We mean you no harm."

"My child is sleeping, so if you can't talk with me from there, then I guess this conversation is over."

Felicia took a step back to close the door. Carmine took off his aviator Ray Bans, and smiled sweetly. "Mrs. Wilson, it's a pleasure to finally meet you. Kenneth talked about you all the time, but his descriptions didn't come close. You are a lovely woman."

A year ago, Felicia would've melted and welcomed them in, but the time with Carolyn helped her be far less trusting.

"Thank you, Mr. Napoli, but I'm in the middle of a few things, so for the last time, how can I help you?"

"It's Carmine, and I apologize for showing up on your doorstep unannounced. You see, your husband is a friend and business associate. We heard about his accident. How is he doing?"

Felicia was losing her patience. "Better. Carmine, what is this about?"

Carmine keyed in on Felicia's body language and decided to postpone the conversation. He continued courteously, but made his message clear. "Mrs. Wilson, this obviously isn't a good time for you. Perhaps we can talk another time. We'll be in touch – have a nice day."

The two men turned and walked under the awning to the 4-door black Maserati. Carmine opened the passenger door, but turned back toward Felicia. "By the way, your roses are beautiful. A little coffee around the roots will help them explode with color. He put his sunglasses back on, and disappeared behind the car door.

Felicia closed the door and leaned against it. What the hell was that? Who were these men, and how did they know Kenneth? Felicia cringed at the thought of having more secrets rise to the surface. This one felt different than the others. This one sent chills down her spine.

Felicia immediately got on the horn to Carolyn, who was running errands, but grabbed some lunch and made a detour to Felicia's place. Felicia prayed Emmanuel would remain asleep long enough for her to brief Carolyn.

"Girl, they didn't give you any idea what they wanted with Kenneth?"

"No, they didn't give up anything, but they were determined to come into the house – at least the big one was."

Carolyn sat her glass on the coffee table and pulled her legs up into the oversized chair. "You know it's probably about some of that dirt Kenneth and Lucas were involved in. There's no telling what they were into, or how deep. What did Mitch say?"

Refusing to make eye contact, Felicia began bagging the trash. "I haven't had time to tell him yet. It happened so fast, and as soon as they left, I called you."

Calmly and politely, Carolyn responded, "Bullshit."

Felicia pretended to be shocked. "What? I did call you as soon as they left!"

"Oh I believe that. I'm calling bullshit on you not having time to call Mitch yet. What were you doing while you were waiting for me to get here?"

"I was..."

"Exactly! Nothing. Nada. You haven't told Mitch yet, because you know he'll tell you exactly what I'm about to tell you. You've got to cut Kenneth loose. Let him know you know about his lies, and you're done with his ass."

Felicia stopped moving.

"Felicia, you're still not ready to do it! Oh, hell, Felicia! We told you not to get involved with his ass again!"

"I'm not, I mean, I didn't...wait..." Felicia plopped on the couch and took a deep breath. "Look Carolyn, I AM DONE with Kenneth! I have no desire to help him with his recovery, but the doctor is saying things could still go south if his emotional state doesn't remain stable."

Carolyn sat up in the chair. "Felicia, who gives a damn about Kenneth's emotional state? Until he decided to pop back from the brink of death, we were all ready to pull the plug, and now you're worried about his emotional state? Hell, tell him, and hopefully he'll relapse and bite the dust, like he should've done months ago!"

"Carolyn!"

"Carolyn what? You know I'm right! Look, you need to tell Mitch. You don't know these men, and you definitely don't know what they're capable of. Tell him Felicia, and stop worrying about Kenneth."

Mitchell was walking through the door just as Carolyn was finishing her sentence. "Tell Mitch what? Hey Carolyn."

"Hey Mitch. Felicia had an interesting day that she NEEDS to tell you about."

Felicia cut Carolyn a dirty look as Mitchell leaned down to kiss her.

"I had visitors – well, Kenneth had visitors today. Wait – what are you doing here this time of day?"

Mitchell was loosening his tie as he sat beside Felicia. "I didn't have any more meetings this afternoon, and figured I could finish my paperwork here. Visitors at the rehab facility?"

"No. Here."

Mitch looked up. "Here? Who – what did they want?"

Carolyn pulled herself up. "Well, my work here is done! Felicia, call me later. Bye Mitch."

"Bye Carolyn. Now what's the deal with these visitors?" Carolyn was out the door before Felicia could get up and walk her to it, so Felicia began explaining.

"It's no big deal. Some men came by looking for Kenneth today. They said they were business associates of his."

Mitchell got comfortable in his seat. "They came by when Carolyn was watching Emmanuel?"

"Carolyn didn't watch Emmanuel. No, they came by after I got back from the rehab center."

"So, you took Emmanuel to see Kenneth?"

Felicia wasn't planning to tell Mitchell about Emmanuel's outing, but the cat was out of the bag. "Yes, but we were only there for a few minutes."

Mitchell's frustration was getting harder to contain. "Felicia, I thought you weren't ready to take him there. Did you talk to Kenneth about the divorce?"

"No, Mitch, I didn't talk to him about ending the marriage. I had the baby with me, he was irritable, and the doctor was talking to me about Kenneth's emotional stability. It just wasn't the right time."

Mitchell closed his eyes and ran his hand through his hair. "Felicia when will it be the right time? He's out of the hospital, he's getting stronger. It appears his brain is working fine. You gotta let the man know your plans. You don't want him having false hope about what his future holds. He's better off knowing the truth."

Felicia tried to make her argument sound logical, but she knew it wouldn't hold up. "Mitch, I told you I'm going to tell him. The doctor wants time to make sure he's strong enough to take it!"

That was it - Mitchell was finished with diplomacy. "Strong enough to take it? What are you talking about? Have you forgotten what this man has done to you – to the other girls? He wasn't worried about your emotional state when he was lying and cheating! Wow - I can't believe this!" Mitchell slid his tie through his collar and tossed it across the room. Felicia was surprised to see Mitchell so aggravated.

"Mitch, why are acting like this? I told you I'm going to do it, I'm just trying to do it right. He is still Emmanuel's father!"

Mitchell was heading to the kitchen for a beer, but stopped and spun in his tracks. "Emmanuel's father? He didn't even want the baby!! Felicia, what are you doing? What are you thinking?"

Mitchell could tell it was time to let it go for now, so he shifted gears and went back for the beer. "Ok, so let's go back to the visitors…"

Felicia knew Mitchell was right about Kenneth and really didn't want to talk anymore, but she knew he wouldn't let this go. "It was no big deal. These two guys came to the house and said they were associates of Kenneth's. When I wouldn't let them in, they said we'd talk again later."

Mitchell made a beeline back to the sofa. "Wait – what? Who were they? They tried to get into the house?"

"No, they didn't try to get in, they just asked if they could come in and talk. The last name was Napoleon, or something like that. They were well dressed, but definitely shady. I'm sure Kenneth was up to no good with them."

Mitchell's tone changed from frustration to concern. "Felicia, you need to remember their names. Lucas could've been just the tip of the iceberg. There's no telling what Kenneth was into. Guys like Kenneth think they're bulletproof, and get in over their heads very easily. If they contact you again, you call me, no matter when or where, got it?"

Felicia knew Mitchell had her best interest at heart, but didn't appreciate him treating her like she was a helpless idiot. "Got it," she replied dryly as she walked out to end the conversation.

As the day rolled into evening, Mitchell stayed in the office working, while Felicia fed Emmanuel before taking him in the back yard for some fresh air. Though they weren't together, Felicia and Mitchell were both in deep thought about the same topic. Felicia was trying to figure out how to discuss her discoveries and divorce with Kenneth, while Mitchell was trying to figure out how to step back and let Felicia handle it. Felicia's thoughts were disrupted by Emmanuel's attempt to chew on a leaf. It was time to put him to bed.

Felicia kissed her sleepy little man goodnight, and slowly closed the nursery door. She knew her next stop had to be the office. As she approached the doorway, she could hear Mitchell talking to himself as he reviewed his spreadsheets.

"Got a minute?" Felicia leaned in the doorway with a hopeful, innocent look.

"For you, of course. Come here." Mitchell was relieved to have the break and hopefully resolve the tension. Felicia strolled around the desk and made herself at home on his lap.

"I'm sorry."

"No, I'm sorry. Look, I care about you so much, and I'm going to be protective of you two. It kills me to think that anyone would want to hurt you. I want you free from the drama, but I do forget sometimes that there is a baby involved." Felicia gave Mitchell a bizarre look and he realized he needed to clarify. "No, I don't forget about E...I mean I'm just really protective of him. I guess I mean, well, I sorta think of him as my son...that's not bad, is it?"

Felicia wrapped her arms around Mitchell's neck and pressed her forehead to his lips. "No, it's not bad at all. Not at all. I'll have the conversation with Kenneth during the next visit."

FIVE

A small ray of sunshine peeked through Felicia's curtains, landing in the perfect spot to force her to open her eyes. She started with one, then the other, squinting throughout. Was this the sign of a better, more normal day? As she turned on her side, her mind drifted far past the back yard furniture, deep into the tall trees. The unknown beyond her property line reminded her of her life. What will she come across next? Will it be a babbling stream full of happy fish and fresh water, or a pack of hungry wolves, each one sizing up a different part of her life to devour? Felicia knew if she thought about it for too long, she wouldn't get out of bed.

Just as she began to rustle, her bedroom door eased open. There, about 3 feet above the doorknob popped Emmanuel's head. He had a toothless, drooling smile from ear to ear, accompanied by Mitchell's Mike Tyson impression.

"Good morning, Mommy! May I come in?"

Felicia chuckled at the lousy ventriloquism act, but played along.

"Well, Good Morning Sweetie! Absolutely, please walk yourself right in here!"

Emmanuel wiggled and squirmed, while Mitchell thought of his next line. "Um, can Uncle Mitch come in too? I walk much better when he's carrying me!"

Mitchell turned Emmanuel into a human airplane and swooped into the room making a soft landing in the center of the bed. Emmanuel didn't wait to be released and eagerly fought his way through the comforter to his mommy. Felicia didn't have to work at it – Emmanuel was strong enough to pull himself up, over the comforter, and into her arms.

"So, Mommy, what is your day looking like?" Mitchell asked as he sat on the edge of the bed while adjusting his full Windsor.

"Well, I'm hoping to make a few calls, and begin getting things in order. I want everything arranged long before he's released, with no surprises."

Mitchell scoffed. "Oh Honey, that's so cute and so naïve. You know there will be surprises. Just expect the unexpected."

As Mitchell finished his sentence, Felicia's phone rang. She looked at the nightstand, then back up at Mitchell. "Was that scripted? Did you plan that?"

Mitchell laughed as Felicia reached for the phone. "No, but so much for your well planned day..."

"Hello?"

"Felicia, it's Jessica."

"Jessica, hey...what's wrong?"

"My mother died last night."

Felicia gasped, which immediately drew Mitchell's attention from wrestling with Emmanuel.

"Oh Jessica, I'm so sorry."

Jessica sounded as if she was still in shock. "I think she knew this was as good as her life would ever be. She was tired. She just gave up."

While Jessica talked, Felicia hopped out of bed, and pulled on a pair of sweat pants.

"Jessica, where are you? Are you at home? It doesn't matter, just tell me where you are and I'm on my way."

Jessica was quiet for a few seconds. "I'm on my way to the funeral home. I've got to make some decisions."

"Let me drop Emmanuel off with a sitter and I'll help. You don't need to be alone right now."

"Felicia, you don't have to do that. I really don't even know why I called you. It's just that we don't have any close family, and it seems like lately I've spent more time with you than anyone else, so I guess that's why you popped into my mind..."

"Jessica, it's fine, really. I'm on my way, and we'll go to the funeral home together, okay?"

"Okay."

Felicia and Carolyn spent the week helping Jessica with the funeral arrangements and removing her mother's things from the nursing home. The days were dark and gloomy, almost as if the sky mourned with Jessica.

Jessica had far fewer relatives than Felicia and Carolyn imagined, so the service was quite intimate – just a few friends and employees from the nursing home. Much to Felicia's surprise, Jessica had no other friends. Felicia wondered what kind of life Jessica had before she met the ladies, but decided to shelve that question for a more appropriate time. Jessica didn't want to go home after the service, so everyone gathered at Felicia's for dinner and a few drinks.

Jessica finally began to open up. "I never thought this day would come. I think I convinced myself that she was getting a little better each day. Maybe I was just getting used to her condition and it was beginning to seem normal to me. It was probably my way of dealing with the guilt."

Felicia interrupted while handing Jessica a scotch. "Stop it – I'm not going to let you beat yourself up about this, especially not today."

Carolyn agreed. "That's right! You didn't do anything. Kenneth did this. You didn't deserve the way he treated you or what he did to your mother. None of it was your fault." Carolyn leaned forward to pour more wine. "Hell, since he's awake, he should be in prison."

A collective sigh was interrupted by Carolyn's brainstorm. "Can we send him to prison?"

Both Carolyn and Jessica turned toward Felicia. Felicia shrugged her shoulders but liked what she was hearing. It would certainly solve her problem. "I don't know...he did cause it, and Jessica, you're a witness."

Jessica flipped her long bangs from her face. "Yeah, but I didn't do anything about it when it happened. There must be some type of timeline on filing a report."

"For abuse maybe, but not for murder," Carolyn stated definitively.

The girls almost appeared hopeful. Felicia felt like the conversation could take dark turn, so decided to shift gears. "I still have Detective Rodriguez's number, and I will call him. But for now, let's concentrate on what you need, Jessica."

Jessica turned toward the window. "The only thing I need is Kenneth's ashes in an urn, just like my mom's."

As days passed, Jessica became more and more intrigued with the possibility of Kenneth's demise. Felicia tried to keep her distracted with visits and outings, but Jessica's determination never wavered. Kenneth was getting better quickly, so Felicia felt it was time to reach out to his parents, and discuss home care options.

Now that Felicia was sure Kenneth was going to recover, she decided it was time to reach out to his family.

"Mr. Wilson? Hi, this is Felicia, Kenneth's wife."

"Hello, Felicia. What can I do for you?"

"I just wanted to touch base and let you know that Kenneth is awake and improving."

"Well, that's great news! I'm very happy to hear it and I'm sure his mother will be too."

"The doctors believe that he has some memory loss, but he's building his strength. They also feel it would do him good to have family around him while he recovers."

"Well now, his mother will be happy to hear that as well. I'll talk to her about scheduling a visit."

"Sounds great. Of course you're welcome to stay here at the house. No need to take on unnecessary expense."

"I appreciate that Felicia. We'll be in touch soon."

Felicia had buttered him up, and it was now time to slap him with the bread. "Mr. Wilson, there is one other thing. During Kenneth's illness, some things came to the surface...some pretty serious things. Kenneth wasn't faithful, and wasn't who I thought he was. When Kenneth is released, we're going to need some time apart to figure this out."

Mr. Wilson could hear how difficult the disclosure was for Felicia, so he let her off the hook. "Felicia, I understand what you're saying, and don't worry – he can come back home with us, until you're ready. His mother will love it. It'll give her something to do. We'll see you in say, a week or two?"

Felicia exhaled with relief. "Yes, thank you so much."

After her conversation with Mr. Wilson, Felicia looked in on Emmanuel. Just as she closed the nursery door, the doorbell rang. It had only been a week since the funeral, but Felicia knew she needed to schedule time with Detective Rodriguez as quickly as possible. Fortunately, he was available on a day when Mitchell had a full schedule.

Felicia opened the door cautiously until she recognized the wavy black hair and serious stance. "Detective, thank you for coming. Please come in – would you like something to drink?"

Detective Rodriguez stepped in carefully and followed Felicia through the entry. He immediately sensed Felicia's anxiety and was eager to hear the purpose of his visit. "No, thank you. How can I help you Felicia?"

"Have a seat, please. Detective, I've got some questions about my husband's past and the potential for legal action."

Detective Rodriguez sat up in his chair. "Go on."

Felicia explained the situation and how Jessica's mother suffered for years before her death. "So, is it possible for Kenneth to be charged with murder? After all, she'd still be alive if it wasn't for Kenneth's actions."

Detective Rodriguez sat still and quiet. He stared at the floor while processing Felicia's story and question. The longer the silence, the more uncomfortable Felicia became.

Detective Rodriguez finally spoke after what felt like a lifetime. "Let me get this straight...your husband, who just miraculously came out of a coma, is now being accused by his current wife of murder? Don't get me wrong – I know he's no saint, but murder?"

"I know this probably sounds crazy, but the more we talked about it, the more ..."

"Wait a minute- the more *who* talked about it?"

"The ex-wives and myself. We recognized that we didn't know enough about the law to pursue it, so I offered to reach out to you."

"Look Mrs. Wilson, if these women were physically abused by this man, they really should've come forward. Unfortunately, there is a statute of limitations regarding how long one has to file those charges. But if this other woman died at his hands, then I think I should look into it – not you and your friends."

Felicia couldn't contain her enthusiasm. "Oh, thank goodness! Thank you Detective! That's the most encouraging news we've heard in a long time."

"You mean, since your husband came out of his coma, right?"

Felicia realized how bizarre her reaction must've sounded and tried to recover. "Detective, it's no surprise to you that I'm no longer a fan of my husband. I'm not going to pretend that I am. I just want justice for my friend."

"Mrs. Wilson, I understand that, but I need you to see this from the perspective of the law. Three women, who feel they've been mistreated by an ex, are now friends and want him charged with murder. Mrs. Wilson, let me give you some advice. Allow us to look into to this, but don't push it. Just know, if anything happens to Kenneth, it won't look good for you."

The detective's warning startled Felicia. After all, she thought she was doing the right thing by bringing Kenneth's behavior forward. "Wait, this man does the things he did, we bring it to your attention, and WE become the suspects? Do you know how many enemies this man probably has?"

The detective rose from his seat, and headed toward the door. "Just tread lightly, Mrs. Wilson. Please let Jessica know I'll be in touch. I'll let myself out."

Felicia sat in disbelief. She knew she needed to pass the detective's warning on to the girls, but it would have to wait. She needed to prepare for the in-laws' visit.

As Felicia pulled into the rehab facility parking lot, she knew this day had the potential for all types of twists and turns. Kenneth's parents had only been in town for a few hours, but were desperate to see him. Mrs. Wilson insisted that Jessica be the one to pick them up from the airport, and take them directly to her baby. The Wilsons didn't know about Jessica's loss only weeks ago, though it probably wouldn't have mattered to Mrs. Wilson anyway. Felicia knew what to expect from Mrs. Wilson, but Jessica was the wild card. How would she react to seeing Kenneth?

Felicia could see Jessica's cherry red sedan in the first row of cars, so she took the long way around to buy a few more minutes. How will Kenneth react when he sees her with his parents? Will he try to lie? Will he relapse? She had no idea what he'd do, but she knew she wouldn't tolerate any level of disrespect, regardless of his health. Jessica and the parents made their way through the double doors as Felicia parked.

Mrs. Wilson was as well put together as the first time Felicia met her. She wore a casual tan pants suit with loafers, her hair in a bun, and that bright red lipstick. Mr. Wilson was a tall, lean man. His head was full of lush, white hair, complete with long sideburns. Kenneth had his facial structure. Mr. Wilson was much more casual than his wife, sporting a golf shirt, jeans, and white tennis shoes.

Based on Felicia's previous encounter with Mrs. Wilson, she felt greeting Mr. Wilson first would be easiest. "Mr. Wilson, I'm Felicia. It's nice to finally meet you. Mrs. Wilson, it's nice to see you again." Mrs. Wilson pretended to be too engulfed in her gazes around the building to speak to Felicia.

Mr. Wilson extended his hand. "Well, it's nice to meet you as well. This is one heck of a hospital."

"It's more of a rehab facility – to get Kenneth back on his feet," Felicia explained.

"Where is he? I want to see him." Mrs. Wilson began heading down a corridor as if she knew exactly where to go.

Felicia stopped her with a stern response. "Wait, Mrs. Wilson. Before we see him, I just want to prepare you."

"Child, he is my baby. I don't need to be prepared to see my own son. Let's go."

"Wait, Mother, hear her out," Mr. Wilson countered.

"Mrs. Wilson, Kenneth has some memory loss. I don't know how much he remembers about anything really. I've asked him and it seems to agitate him. I'm saying this because he may not remember that he never told us about each other. He may not even remember you two."

"That's ridiculous, I'm his mother! He'll remember me. And maybe he's chosen to block out parts of his past for a reason, Felicia! Jessica, lead the way."

Jessica's name was the first word she heard. "Oh, I'm not going in with you."

"Now, Jessica, I know you mentioned not feeling well, but I'm sure Kenny would be happy to see you. Come on."

"No, Mrs. Wilson, I'm not going in. I've got some things to take care of, and I'll meet you back at Felicia's for dinner later." Jessica turned and headed through the doors before Mrs. Wilson could respond. Felicia was relieved – one less thing to worry about.

"This way…" Felicia led the folks down the hall and around the corner to Kenneth's room. Felicia went in first, primarily to see the expression on his face without obstruction. Kenneth turned away from his TV program to see Felicia approaching. He beamed. "Hi."

Felicia spoke with a more solemn tone. "Hi. Kenneth, I have someone with me."

Before Felicia could complete her thought, Mrs. Wilson pushed past her and dove into Kenneth's chest.

"My Kenny! Oh, my baby! Lord, I didn't know if I'd ever see those beautiful eyes of yours again. Thank goodness!"

Kenneth was stunned. "Mom?"

"Yes baby, yes, it's your Mama. Your father is here too. And I'm not letting you out of my sight again for a very long time."

Kenneth smiled over his mother's head at his dad, then over at Felicia. Felicia wanted to monitor Kenneth's true response so she smiled approvingly in silence.

Mr. Wilson walked over to the bed and gently patted Kenneth's head. "It's good to see you son."

"You too, Dad. Are you staying at our house?"

Mr. Wilson looked back at Felicia to field the question, since Mrs. Wilson declined the invitation. Felicia obliged. "Kenneth, your parents decided to get some rest at a hotel, but may migrate back to the house later during their visit." Felicia walked around to the opposite side of the room and sat at the foot of the bed. It was time to let him in on the plan. "Look, Kenneth, you're getting better. You're progressing much faster than the doctor expected. I've chatted with your parents and we agree that you're going to need more help and attention than I can give you - you know, with Emmanuel crawling now. We think it would be best if you go back with them to continue your recovery."

A hush fell over the room as they watched Kenneth process what he heard. He took a deep breath. "I guess if you guys think it makes sense. You guys trust each other, and I trust you." It was obvious that Kenneth didn't remember never introducing the three of them. Before Felicia could continue, Mrs. Wilson cut her off.

"Of course it makes sense, baby. You need time with your Mama, eating my cooking and letting your father and me nurse you back to good health."

Kenneth turned back to Felicia. "Okay, well then, I'll go back with them, and I'll be back as soon as I can."

Felicia felt her expression change, but she knew she couldn't tip Kenneth off in front of his parents. "We'll talk about that later. Right now, you focus on getting well. You guys visit, and I'll be right back."

Felicia rounded the corner and forced herself against the wall, panting as if she'd run miles. Kenneth didn't even realize he was busted. How could she tell him she didn't want him back if he didn't understand his past?

While the family enjoyed their reunion, Felicia decided to run to her favorite diner to pick up dinner.

Though she called in the order, The Southern Fried Diner didn't have the food ready. Felicia didn't mind, because it allowed her a few minutes to strategize.

Dinner in hand, Felicia headed through the parking lot and off to pick up the in-laws, when she heard her name.

"Felicia – Mrs. Wilson, is that you?"

Felicia turned around to see Carmine Napoli approaching. His tailored slacks and starched white shirt were worth more than the average weekly salary. Carmine had a warm smile and smooth stroll, but it was clear that he was trouble.

"Felicia, what a surprise!" How are you, and that precious little boy of yours? Again my apologies for showing up uninvited."

"We're fine. What are you doing here, Carmine?"

"I'm guessing the same as you. This place has the best peach cobbler in town. I'll travel anywhere for good food. So, how's your husband?"

Felicia was nervous but knew she couldn't show it, so she channeled Carolyn.

"Mr. Nap - Carmine, it's obvious that you and my husband had some very serious business dealings, and I'm guessing that my husband hasn't held up his end of the deal. Can we please avoid this dance and you tell me what you want from us-I mean, him?"

Carmine smiled with approval. "Felicia, you got moxie. I like that. I like you. Yes, I am one of your husband's business associates, and yes, our business transactions are not complete. I understand he's still on the mend and will be out soon. I just want to make sure he hasn't forgotten about me."

Felicia looked puzzled. "How did you know he would be out soon?"

Carmine politely ignored Felicia's question. He reached into his pants pocket and Felicia tensed up.

"Felicia, here's my card. I own a few dry cleaners downtown. If you need anything, please don't hesitate to call. Here's a second one. Give it to your husband." Carmine smiled sweetly, and though Felicia was tempted to smile back, she couldn't. A black Lexus sedan pulled up just as Carmine turned away. He casually climbed into the back seat, and off they went.

Felicia's logic told her she should be afraid, but for some reason, she wasn't. Carmine was obviously a powerful man, but he just didn't seem like the type to hurt women and children. She quickly remembered that her instincts had been wrong before, and a chill rushed down her spine. Felicia trotted to her car, jumped in, and locked the door.

SIX

"Mr. Wilson, did you get enough to eat?" Felicia inquired.

""Oh yes, yes I did. Thank you so much for such a nice meal. I've always enjoyed fish, but it's always better when I'm near the ocean. It may not be true, but I feel like they went fishing especially for me!" Mr. Wilson chuckled as he dropped his napkin in his plate and leaned back from the table to give his round waistline a little room to breathe.

Felicia smiled. "I know exactly what you mean. Mrs. Wilson, can I get you anything?"

Mrs. Wilson was very quiet throughout the meal, only speaking when spoken to. "No, thank you. We hate to eat and run, but we've got a big day tomorrow, making arrangements to take Kenny home and such. We need to make our way on to the hotel and check in before it gets too late. Thank you for dinner Felicia. Jessica, are you ready to take us back?"

Jessica was in a bit of a daze, and didn't hear the conversation.

"I'm sorry – what were you saying?"

Mr. Wilson spoke up. "Now Mother, it would be rude to just run off. Felicia hasn't even cleared the table yet and you're running out the door. And maybe Jessica would like a few minutes to let her food digest. I know I would."

"I can take you whenever you're ready," Jessica added, not hearing the statement before but assuming her response was a safe bet.

Felicia whined, "Oh, I wish you two would stay here. There's plenty of room and it would give you more time with your grandson."

Mrs. Wilson had already left the table and was heading into the family room to gather her things. Emmanuel rolled himself over and upright in the playpen so he could see who was crossing his path. He watched her movements, but watched in silence.

Mrs. Wilson ignored Felicia's appeal. "I'm sure Jessica is ready to go. Jessica honey, it was very kind of you to endure this dinner for us."

"Endure??" Jessica and Felicia responded in harmony.

Mrs. Wilson looked puzzled. "Well, yes. I mean, come on, I know this had to be awkward for you, but being the considerate girl you are, you sat through it for us. You were always a considerate girl."

Jessica had been checked out for the majority of the evening, but was now completely engaged. "Mrs. Wilson, I didn't *endure* anything. I didn't endure dinner, I enjoyed it. This isn't my first time having dinner with Felicia."

Mrs. Wilson turned back toward Felicia as they migrated into the family room. "Why on earth would you be doing that? I mean, what reason could you possibly have for spending time with the woman who stole your husband? No offense, Felicia."

But offense was taken. "No offense? Look, Mrs. Wilson, I didn't steal Jessica's husband. I had no idea Kenneth was married when I met him."

Mrs. Wilson had egged Felicia on and was thrilled she took the bait. "Didn't know? How could you possibly not know the man was married? Kenny loved Jessica with every breath he took. He was a devoted husband, even letting Jessica's mother move in with them. I'm sure he wasn't available to you all day and night like your other male friends. That should've been a clue."

Felicia could feel her face getting warm. She tried desperately not to dignify Mrs. Wilson's comments with a response, but couldn't help it. Felicia had to ensure she didn't say something she would regret.. "Kenneth was around more than any man I ever knew, and wasn't forthcoming about anything, including his marriage to Jessica." . She knew Jessica didn't need to be pulled into this, but she simply couldn't allow the bullying.

Mr. Wilson had his fill as well. "Mother, stop it. This woman opened her home to us. She shared a very nice dinner and offered us a place to lay our heads. You are being disrespectful!" Mr. Wilson turned toward Felicia who had made her way to Emmanuel's playpen. "Felicia, maybe we should head to the hotel."

Mrs. Wilson wasn't interested in Mr. Wilson's comments or his suggestion to leave. "Oh, no. Now, I think I need my food to settle." Mrs. Wilson sat in the chair next to the playpen and smiled at Emmanuel as Felicia scooped him out. Emmanuel still wasn't impressed with her and turned away.

"This is what I know; my son was strong, sweet, smart and ambitious. He was head over heels for Jessica and happily married until he met you. Suddenly, he dropped off the face of the earth, divorced, shacked up with you, and almost died. Now, from where I sit, the only thing that changed in his life, was meeting you! And poor, sweet Jessica. I know she's too sweet and classy to get into the mud to fight for her man, no matter how good he was to her."

Mr. Wilson begged but was ignored, "Mother, please..."

"Jessica, I know you're too sweet and docile to get into that kind of fight. Plus, once a man is encouraged to stray by another woman, it's hard to reel them back in. Sometimes, they even threaten the wife. Honey, did she threaten you?"

Felicia couldn't hold back. "Of course I didn't' threaten her! That's absolutely ridiculous! Look, Jessica and I have talked through everything and now have a solid relationship – actually friendship, and we both agree that Kenneth does and did whatever he wanted, without any pressure from anyone else!"

Mr. Wilson was trying to head toward the entry, but Mrs. Wilson hadn't moved. "Now that's just the craziest thing I've ever heard! An ex-wife and current wife being friends? Especially after what you put this sweet girl through?"

"Mother, that's enough! Felicia, I am so sorry. Thank you for..."

"No! I have wondered why my son disappeared out of my life and now I have a chance to hear from the source. I want an answer. Felicia, you're a decent looking girl. Why would you go after someone else's husband and keep him from his family? Kenny was always a family man, and wouldn't change so much without some influence from someone else."

That was the last straw. Jessica snapped, "Stop it! Just stop it! And don't you dare call me sweet Jessica again!"

"Jessica, what on earth are you upset about? Honey, I'm defending you!"

"Defending me? From what? I don't need defending now – I needed it back when your perfect son was throwing me around the house!"

Both Mr. and Mrs. Wilson stopped moving.

"That's right – your wonderful, perfect son was beating me!"

Mrs. Wilson dismissed Jessica's accusation. "Jessica honey, what on earth are you talking about?"

Felicia knew Jessica had years of frustration just begging to come out, and feared it was on its way. "Jessica, you don't have to do this. Don't let her push your buttons."

"Yes Felicia, I do need to do this! I've needed to do this for a long time – doing this is way past due!"

Jessica turned to Mrs. Wilson. "You're sitting here, blaming Felicia for my divorce when you have no idea what happened!"

"Now, Jess..."

"No Mrs. Wilson, it's my turn to talk now!"

Mrs. Wilson sat back in her seat, stunned.

"Felicia didn't know about me, and she didn't know about you because your perfect son was a master at lying, both blatantly, and through omission. Don't get me wrong, something was obviously wrong with me because I married him, but you didn't know him at all! Your son had no interest in being faithful, and got to a point where he didn't even care if I knew. He was a mean man, and a meaner drunk, and trust me, he drank plenty!"

The room was silent and the occupants were as still as the furniture. Even Emmanuel stopped squirming in his mother's arms.

"Kenneth was great at putting on a show for his adoring public, but behind closed doors, anything, and I do mean anything, could set him off. Closed fist, open fist – it didn't matter to him, and it definitely didn't matter that I was half his size, not to mention a woman. Yes, my mother stayed with us, but it definitely wasn't his choice. I had to beg him to let her stay because she had nowhere else to go. And I used the possibility of having him arrested for the abuse as a bargaining chip. If I had the guts to go to the police, she'd still be alive."

The parents held their breath in fear of Jessica's next words. She saw their faces and answered the unasked question.

"Your crazy, narcissistic son killed my mother!" Felicia rocked Emmanuel, comforting herself more than the baby. Her heart was breaking for Jessica.

"He pushed her down a flight of stairs. He didn't mean to hurt her. He was trying to get his hands on me and she jumped between us."

Mr. and Mrs. Wilson stared at each other in stunned silence. Tears began to well in Mrs. Wilson's eyes as Mr. Wilson made his way back to the sofa.

"She didn't die right away, but she was never the same, until..." Jessica couldn't catch her breath, so Felicia finished the thought.

"Jessica's mom just passed away a few weeks ago." Jessica trotted to the bathroom down the hall.

Mrs. Wilson put her hand over her heart and shook her head in disbelief. "This can't be true. It just can't be true."

Felicia confirmed, "It's true. Kenneth has done some unthinkable things to all three of us."

Mrs. Wilson sat up. "The THREE of you? Oh, well, if you're including Carolyn, then I'm not sure how credible any of this is. That woman had problems from the moment Kenneth met her."

"Mrs. Wilson, stop it. You can't blame Carolyn for Kenneth's behavior. We all lived through some version of this nightmare. Though the details were different, his general behavior was the same. I planned to tell you all of this, I just wasn't planning to tell you tonight. That's why I wanted him to go with you to work on his recovery. Kenneth hasn't been very nice to me either, and I learned to blame myself for his rage. Though he hasn't put his hands on me yet, I truly believe it was coming." Felicia paused, dropping her head. "Wow, that's the first time I said it out loud. Before his accident, he was becoming more and more aggressive. I never imagined it could happen to me, until I met Carolyn and Jessica. You need to know that I'm planning to divorce him as soon as he's considered competent by the doctors. He may have never planned to lay a hand on me, but I don't want to take that chance, and I definitely don't want my child growing up around that behavior. And if you're worried about his heart being broken, don't. He shouldn't be too torn up about it. After all, I was nothing but a mark for Kenneth anyway – a way of getting money."

Jessica came out of the bathroom with fully restored makeup, but swollen, red eyes. She walked over to Felicia and pulled Emmanuel into her arms.

"We've been spending time together, and realize we have more in common than just Kenneth. We all had something in our lives that rocked our self-esteem. Something in our pasts made us believe we were defective in some way, and we had to find our value in a man – any man. We didn't realize it at the time, but something deep down made us believe we didn't deserve anything better. Yes, even tough-talking Carolyn. Kenneth treated us the way he did, because he saw that he could. He exploited us to avoid his own self esteem issues. Honestly, I wish we had pulled the plug when we had the chance. He's got one more relationship coming, and her name is Karma. And I just might be the one to introduce them."

Jessica gently kissed Emmanuel's forehead and handed him back to Felicia. She was calm and collected. It was as if she had purged a lifetime of pain. "Ready to go?"

The Wilsons were still sitting in silence. They had no idea what to do with the information they were given. Mr. Wilson stood up first, took a deep breath, and ran his hand through his wavy hair. He walked over to his wife and helped her rise slowly. While she fumbled with her purse, Mr. Wilson made his way to Felicia. He gently rubbed Emmanuel's head, then gripped Felicia's arm and kissed her forehead. He could feel his emotions getting the best of him, so he quickly moved toward the entry. Mrs. Wilson wouldn't look at Felicia. She slowly turned and walked past her husband, and out the door.

Felicia needed to warn Jessica about her conversation with Detective Rodriguez. "Jessica, I'll call you later tonight."

The ladies embraced. "No need, Felicia, I'm fine. I'll call you tomorrow."

Felicia whispered, "Jessica, listen to me. I talked to the detective. I don't know if they'll be able to charge Kenneth with your mother's murder, but you have to stay calm and steer clear. Don't do anything – not to Kenneth, and not to yourself. Just let the police handle it. Either way, he'll be out of our lives soon, I promise."

Jessica showed no emotion. "Good night, Felicia."

SEVEN

Bills, bills, bills. Felicia shuffled the bills around on the desk, as if they would dissolve into the wood. Kenneth's insurance policy covered his medical expenses, but very little else. It was clear that Felicia would have to sell the house. She knew her relationship with Mitchell was serious, but she didn't want him to feel obligated to save her home. Besides, if she sold the house, Felicia could also pay off Kenneth's death to Carmine, and never have to see him again. That's what she'd do. Felicia was proud she made a decision. She was also pretty hungry, so the best thing to do before heading back to the bills was to grab a burger and get a little fresh air. She twisted her hair into a loose bun, scooped Emmanuel out of the playpen, and off they went.

As she headed back home to complete her task, Felicia brainstormed. Kenneth always managed the money, but since they would be parting ways, she could no longer be just a homemaker. Maybe it was time to return to her career of teaching. Could she do it? Felicia always worked at the middle school level, and loved the creative freedom she had with the curriculum. The ideas danced in her mind all the way home. She couldn't wait to devour her lunch and share her idea with Mitchell.

Emmanuel finally gave into his afternoon nap, which gave Felicia the perfect opportunity to chat. She called Mitchell.

"Hey Honey, do you have a few minutes to talk?"

"Actually Felicia, I was planning to touch base with you too. I'm headed your way now. Almost there."

Mitchell's voice caused concern for Felicia. "Ok, I'll see you shortly." She was so distracted by Mitchell's tone, she didn't notice Emmanuel's favorite bear until it was under her foot. The soft bear slid across the hardwood floor, taking Felicia with it. She went down hard. She squirmed as she fell, attempting to avoid the end table, but her cheek caught its metal corner and propelled her into the wall. Felicia sat slumped against the wall, a bit dazed. What just happened? She inspected herself, starting with her legs. Though she was sitting at a strange angle, she was able to move. Nothing appeared to be broken, but she decided to stay where she landed for a few minutes to compose herself.

It seemed like only seconds when she heard Mitchell unlocking the door. Felicia began scrambling to pull herself up, but a pain shot down from her hip, and she returned to her spot against the wall.

"Felicia? Felicia!" When Mitchell spotted Felicia on the floor, he dove to her rescue. "What happened? Are you hurt? Oh my God, Felicia, your face is bleeding!"

Felicia felt her cheek throbbing, but didn't realize the table cut her. "I'm okay, really. I just slipped on one of Emmanuel's toys."

"You don't look okay," Mitchell said as he scanned Felicia's body. "Can you move?"

"Yes Honey, I'm fine – really. I just need a little boost. And I'm sure the cut looks worse than it really is."

Before Felicia could pull her legs underneath her, Mitchell scooped her up and placed her gently on the sofa. "Don't move. I'll be right back. We need to clean that cut."

As Mitchell wiped away the blood and patched her up, Felicia began sharing her idea.

"I'm thinking about going back to work. I was going through the bills, and even if I sell the house, I'll need to work. I want to work. I miss it."

Mitchell appeared focused on his bandaging, but was listening to every word. "What brought this on?"

"Mitch, I'm going broke. This house is a beast to keep up, and it doesn't make sense for me to sit around when I could be working. I never wanted to stop. That was all Kenneth's idea."

"I told you I would help you with the finances. Felicia, if you want to work, that's fine. But you don't have to. You just need to cut Kenneth loose and we can move forward."

Felicia leaned away from Mitchell's touch. "Mitchell, I appreciate you wanting to help, but I don't need you to rescue me. I can work. There is no reason for me to stay at home. Emmanuel is old enough to spend a few hours a day in daycare, and I know Carolyn would love to help out. And by the way, if cutting Kenneth loose was that easy, I would've done it by now. I've got a plan for getting rid of Kenneth and I've got to stick to it."

"Felicia, what the hell does that mean? Okay, I mean, I get that you have a plan, but Baby, you've got to admit, this whole thing feels like it's dragging. I need to feel like we're making some progress here."

Felicia was getting angry. "Mitch, what are you doing? Why are you pressuring me about this? Are you trying to end this, end us?"

"Felicia, stop. Listen, you know how I feel about you and E. I couldn't love you more if I tried. And I know without hesitation, that you'll be a part of my life for the rest of my life. But Felicia, I seem to want more from you than you're able to give right now. You've got so much going on, and though I try to help you through this, you just won't let me. I don't feel included in your decisions at all."

"Mitch, I do include you! I asked you to spend your time here with us. I tell you about our days and the craziness that's going on around me! You are totally included in everything!"

"Felicia, you talk about what's going on, but you're only reporting the information, not including me in the decision making or allowing me to help. You won't let me help you with the bills, and you didn't even tell me about the dinner with Kenneth's parents."

"I did tell you!"

"Felicia, you volunteered no information. When I finally asked, you just said it wasn't great. I don't even know the outcome."

Felicia wasn't sure if she had told him or not, so she seized the moment. "His parents are back home and will take him as soon as he's released, and he agreed to it."

Mitchell sighed, "Look, you've been through hell, and you need someone you can trust. Someone who is completely in your corner and can help you get through this. To be honest, I feel like you're spending a lot more time with Kenneth than what's expected of you. You talk about your conversations and time there, and it really doesn't sound like a woman who wants a divorce."

Felicia no longer felt the pain of her injuries. "Oh, come on Mitchell, not this again. Look, I appreciate you wanting to help me, but right now, I don't even know what I need help with. Mitch, I love you. I'm planning to be with you. I admit, Kenneth is becoming more like the man I knew before he and I got married, and it does make things easier. It doesn't mean I want him back, and it certainly doesn't mean I trust him again. I still have no idea how many other shady deals he was involved in, and I'm not interested in finding out."

"Funny you should mention that…you know, after Carmine showed up on your doorstep, I began to wonder how we could find out more about him, so I visited Lucas last week."

"You did what??" Felicia slapped Mitchell's hand from her face. "Mitch, why on earth would you see Lucas? After everything I went through with him, why would you give him the time of day?"

"Felicia, we needed answers, and Lucas could provide them. Carmine is not a nice guy. He's involved in some really heavy stuff. This is not a man you want to cross."

Felicia was officially offended. "Mitch, I'm not planning any dinner parties in Carmine's honor. I'm not stupid – I know he's dangerous."

"You only think you know. Lucas said Carmine was a part of their diamond import business. Carmine was fencing the stones that Lucas and Kenneth brought into the country. Apparently, Carmine paid for a shipment that never arrived. Lucas says he gave them to Kenneth, and Kenneth was supposed to deliver to Carmine's associates, but never did. Shortly after that, Kenneth had the accident. Lucas said Carmine may have had something to do with that too. The last person that didn't pay Carmine what he owed was found in the alligator pit at the city zoo. Well, they didn't find him, but they found his shredded clothes and enough teeth to identify him with dental records. And now, Lucas is livid and paranoid because Carmine wants him dead too. Lucas thinks Kenneth owes Carmine well into six figures. Felicia, this man could easily come after you."

Felicia was terrified but chose to turn the tables on Mitchell. "I still can't believe you went to see Lucas without telling me. You went behind my back! That man ruined my life and you're spending time with him? How am I supposed to trust you when you're sneaking around, having secret meetings?"

Mitchell was floored that Felicia kept avoiding his point. "Felicia, I'm not sneaking around, and it was Kenneth that ruined your life, not Lucas!" Mitchell scooted away from Felicia and stood up. "See? This is exactly what I mean! You're already letting Kenneth off the hook. You're in a lot deeper with him than you think you are. You need to admit you still care for him."

"Mitchell, Kenneth has brain damage! He hardly remembers his life, much less his crimes! And of course I care for him! He's my husband! We have a life together!"

Mitchell dropped his head. "There it is. He's still your husband. You still describe him in the present tense. Felicia, I love you. But as long as you still believe you have a life with Kenneth, there's no place here for me." Mitchell walked up to Felicia, cupped her face and kissed her gently. "I'll always be here for you, Felicia, but I think I need to stay at my place for a while, or at least until you're ready to confront Kenneth."

Felicia panicked. "Mitch, you misunderstood me! I meant that we had a life together! You and I have a life together now!

I'm just trying to get him out of here so we can move forward! There's no need for you go!"

Mitchell was calm, but obviously hurt. "I'll be around. And if you need me for anything, I'll be here in a heartbeat. But right now, I think I'm just a distraction. Take care of yourself, and please be careful dealing with Carmine. He's a dangerous man. I'll talk with you later. Put some ice on that hip." Mitchell picked up his keys and left.

As Mitchell pick up his keys from the bar, Felicia moaned, "Mitchell, wait. Please don't do this."

Mitchell glanced back briefly but kept moving toward the entry. "Don't worry baby, I'll be back when you're ready."

A slamming door would've made Mitchell's departure easier to swallow, but his gentle demeanor as he carefully closed and locked the door from the outside sent Felicia over the edge. As she sat, sniffing and wiping away tears, Felicia refused to buy into anything Mitchell said, and was determined to prove him wrong. How could he accuse her of still caring for Kenneth? It was important for Kenneth to be well before she confronted him. That was her logic. But was Mitchell right? Was she stalling? Was she falling for Kenneth again? Was she falling for his change in demeanor, his sudden kindness, and him needing her? It didn't matter. It couldn't matter. If she didn't want to lose Mitchell, Felicia had to walk away. She had to tell Kenneth what she knew.

EIGHT

Felicia took the evening to determine her approach with Kenneth. Felicia wasn't a cruel person, and in spite of the conversation, she still wanted to be mature about it. After all, Kenneth was Emmanuel's father, and would still be a part of his life. She'd still have to deal with him long after this drama was over.

As she showered and dressed, Felicia ached from her fall. She now had a large purple bruise peeking around the edges of her bandage, and the tissue around her eye had swollen. Not a pretty picture. But she knew if she postponed the conversation another day, she'd be accused of stalling and lose Mitchell for good. She dropped Emmanuel off with Carolyn, and headed to the rehab facility. Carolyn wouldn't let her leave until she provided a convincing explanation for the cuts and bruises, but was clear that the conversation would be continued later.

When Felicia arrived, the nurses refused to let her see Kenneth until they examined her. They told her how to take care of her bruised hip, and even changed her bandage, complimenting Mitchell's handiwork. They even wheeled her into Kenneth's room so she wouldn't have to limp down the long corridor.

"You have a visitor," Jennifer announced, as she wheeled her into Kenneth's room. Kenneth turned toward the door. He was startled by Felicia's appearance. "No, no, no..." he whimpered.

The nurse locked Felicia's wheels and exited, closing the door behind her.

"Felicia, what happened?"

"Nothing. We'll talk about it later. Look Kenneth, I need to share some things with you. You may or may not remember it, but we need to talk about it. Look, before your accident, things weren't great with us. We had some problems. I thought we had the potential to work them out, but..."

"Felicia, what happened? Who did this to you?"

"Kenneth, while you were in your coma, some things came to light about us. About you."

"What kinds of things?" Kenneth drug his hands through his hair.

"Well, first I couldn't make any decisions about you without talking with Carolyn and Jessica. You didn't change your legal documents after we got married."

Kenneth looked puzzled. "I didn't? Felicia, I know I don't remember everything, but that doesn't make sense."

"I know. Anyway, the more time the three of us spent together, the more I learned about the person you had been. I even found out that your parents were alive, Kenneth. And they had no idea I existed."

"Of course my parents are alive. You know that. You've known that since we met."

Felicia countered, "No Kenneth. You told me they were dead. The first I learned of your parents' existence was while you were in the hospital."

Kenneth looked lost and confused. "Felicia, that doesn't make sense. Why would I keep my parents from you? What would I have to gain from doing that? You're not making sense."

It was clear that this conversation was going to take some time, so Felicia dropped her purse on the floor and took a deep breath. "You kept a lot from me, Kenneth, including your diamond import business."

Kenneth chuckled. "My what? Come on Felicia. This is crazy. A diamond business? If I was working with diamonds, I think I'd remember something about it, don't you?"

"I don't know Kenneth. The doctors said you experienced some pretty serious brain trauma, and it's hard to tell what you retained about your life. Kenneth, you weren't a good person. I thought you were, but the longer you stayed unconscious, the more I found out. Anyway, when you're strong enough to travel, your parents are going to take you back home with them."

Kenneth smiled and shook his head in agreement. "I know. You told me, and I think it's a good idea. You don't need me around until I'm strong enough to help you with my little man."

Felicia leaned forward in the chair as her voice dropped an octave. "Kenneth, you're not coming back home, at least not back to me."

"What are you talking about Felicia?"

"Kenneth, you didn't love me. You were only with me because you needed money and a life that appeared legitimate. I was your mark, Kenneth."

"My mark? Okay, now you're just talking crazy Felicia. Why on earth would I need a mark?"

"You hurt Jessica's mother badly, and you had to take care of her, so you needed money. You managed our finances, so I never realized how much you'd taken from my savings, and you got involved with Lucas and the diamonds. Who you were, what you did, and our relationship was all a big lie."

Kenneth looked shocked to hear Lucas's name. "Lucas? Okay, I've heard enough. The beating those guys gave you obviously rattled your brain. This is all ridiculous. I think you need to head home and rest. We can talk more when you feel better."

Felicia had come too far to stop now. "No, Kenneth. I'm fine, and you may not want to hear this, but I need to say it. I wish you well but I can't be with you anymore. I can't go back to the world where I was ignorant to your dealings and how you felt about me. I just can't. I'll be filing for divorce." Felicia paused, looking off into the distance. "Wait – why did you assume someone beat me up?"

Kenneth ignored the question. "Felicia, how can I defend myself when I don't even remember any of this? It sounds like you're overreacting to some exaggerated stories that some jealous, manipulative idiots filled your head while I was unconscious. Besides, you know me better than anyone. Do you really think I was capable of all of that? Hell, I'm not even smart enough to pull off that kind of crap."

Felicia repeated the question. "Why did you assume someone beat me up?"

Kenneth stammered, "Well, what else could it be? I mean, you come in all bandaged up, and…"

Felicia cut him off. "I fell. I tripped on a toy and I fell." She stared deeply into Kenneth's darting eyes. The real Kenneth was back. "Wow, you do remember. I need to go."

Kenneth leaned forward, and yelled, "Felicia wait! Please don't let the ramblings of some scorned tramps destroy what we had!"

Felicia remained composed. "Kenneth, Jessica's mother is dead. She died from the injuries you caused. These aren't the ramblings of scorned tramps. I've listened to the stories. I've seen the diamonds, and I've met some of your associates – by the way, Carmine sends his regards. Look, I don't know what you remember and what you don't but I know just can't stay in this marriage another minute, and it doesn't have anything to do with anyone but you."

Kenneth folded his arms, attempting not to react to hearing Carmine's name. "So what happens next, Felicia? You allow these strangers to continue to influence you? You let them talk you into breaking up your family? Raising your son alone? You know I'm not having that, Felicia."

Felicia refused to let Kenneth rattle her. "I'm smarter than that Kenneth. And I'm not alone. Jessica and Carolyn are two amazing women, and they've really helped me get through this. The only person I don't need is you."

"Don't fall for their antics, Felicia. They're both a couple of selfish drama queens! Our life was a good one, until the accident. Keeping the exes on the paperwork was a stupid oversight, and what the hell do I know about fencing some damned blood diamonds?"

Felicia was focused on rising carefully from the wheelchair until Kenneth mentioned the gems. "Fencing blood diamonds?"

"Yes! You see how ridiculous it sounds when you say it?"

Felicia smiled slightly. "No, that's not it. I said you were involved in a diamond import business – not fencing, and I didn't say anything about Africa."

Kenneth tried to backtrack. "Well, where else do diamonds come from? That's just the first place I thought of –"

"Stop, Kenneth. Just stop it. You do remember. You remember everything, don't you?"

Kenneth's face changed from confusion to pure evil. "Why Felicia, what are you gonna do? Are you gonna run to the police? Maybe call that detective who arrested Lucas?"

Felicia gulped.

"That's right, Felicia, you haven't been my only visitor. You know, this would've been much easier if you just remained the mousey, worried wife. I'd get well, we'd raise the baby and live happily ever after.

"Kenneth, how did you know about Lucas? When did it all start coming back to you?"

Kenneth smirked. "Well, if you must know, I've had it all along. Even when I couldn't speak and you were the faithful wife, helping me with physical therapy, cheering me on, even grooming me. You made me look good all over again, and you enjoyed it – I could tell. "I even remembered our past right away. When I met you, you were a very pretty, innocent girl. You weren't gorgeous, but pretty enough for me to be seen with you. You tried so hard to appear confident and strong, but I saw right through it. I saw the frightened little girl."

"Oh my gosh. Kenneth, what kind of person…"

"Oh Felicia, don't take it the wrong way. This is why I chose you. You made it so easy for me. Don't get me wrong, I really liked you. At times, I even think I loved you, because you made it so easy for me. I smiled my smile, and you'd melt. I gave you a little attention, and you gave in completely. And when I proposed, you jumped at the chance. You were everything I needed, and just gullible enough to believe whatever I told you. And hey, there was no need to introduce you to my parents because I didn't plan for you to be around this long."

Felicia couldn't move. "You bastard! I gave you all of me! I had a baby with you!"

Kenneth glanced out the window. "Yeah, that whole baby thing wasn't a part of the plan. I was actually hoping you couldn't get pregnant."

"So what was the plan when I did get pregnant? Beat me to the point of miscarriage like you did to Carolyn?" Felicia barked.

Kenneth shook his head. "I can't even imagine what that bitch told you. She was crazy when I met her. I'm really quite surprised you two got along well enough to share stories. You two have nothing in common – except me, of course."

"I also met your mistress," Felicia added. "She spent plenty of time beside your hospital bed. I see why you've stayed with her so long. She hadn't been beaten yet."

"Felicia, you give me far too much credit. There was no way I could've kept that relationship going through three marriages. She came and went as I pleased. Just a distraction from you three. She knew how to obey." Kenneth leaned in and chuckled, "Don't tell her, but we have absolutely no future together."

"Do you think this is funny? Do you think this is a game, Kenneth? You lied, you cheated, you abused women. You almost died, and still have no remorse? Don't you feel anything about how you treated Carolyn or Jessica? What about Jessica's mother? You killed a woman!"

Kenneth leaned back comfortably. "Jessica was another weakling. And if her bitch of a mother wasn't always in our business, she wouldn't have gotten hurt. That wasn't my fault. I didn't go after her – she came after me."

"She died from the injuries you caused! You pushed her down the stairs!"

Kenneth glanced out the window, then back to Felicia. "Yes, that was unfortunate."

"A glimpse of compassion?"

"Oh no, not at all. It's unfortunate for Jessica, because now her gravy train is gone, I'm free."

Felicia couldn't take it. "You murdered that woman! It may have taken a while for her to die, but she died from the injuries you caused! You could spend the rest of your sorry life in prison, if Jessica doesn't get to you first. She wants you dead!"

Kenneth casually raised his arms and rested his hands behind his head. "Oh, Felicia, you are so naïve. That accident happened a million years ago, and I assume Jessica told you she never called the police. How on earth do you expect her to be able to connect me to her mom's death now? And as for her wanting me dead...well, let's just say Jessica's threats are really low on my list of concerns."

Felicia stood strong. "You're going to pay for everything you've done to us, Kenneth, mark my words."

Kenneth looked surprised. "Done to you? The only thing I've done to you is make your life worth living. I mean, let's be honest - you really didn't even exist before me. As with everything Felicia, there was a price of admission. You were happy until my accident. And of all of the homely little tramps I spent time with for the sake of my business, you were my favorite. Anyway, good luck proving any of this, including this conversation. You see, I suffered a major brain injury, and I've lost a huge part of my past. How easy will it be to find a jury that will convict a man with no memory of his sins? Oh, and if you're thinking about having more conversations with the police about my diamond business, please let them know that Lucas handled anything that could be traced. Poor, dumb Lucas. All that time in law school, and not a lick of common sense."

Kenneth's arrogance was now in overdrive. "Now, why don't you be a good girl and get the house ready for me to come home? You see, my wife, I'm coming home in just a few days. Oh Felicia, apparently the doctor hadn't told you the good news yet."

"Wait, what? Oh, no you aren't. You're going home with your parents and I'm divorcing you, Kenneth, and you're never setting foot in that house again."

"Again, so gullible. That house isn't ours Darling, it's mine. Don't you remember? The house is in my name. So when you divorce me, I'm not moving out – you are. When we bought it, you weren't interested in all of the paperwork, so I added a short document stating that in the event of a split, you relinquish all rights to the home. And guess what – you signed it. I'm coming home, with or without you, Felicia."

Felicia quickly hobbled to the door, turning back before she crossed the threshold. "You won't make it home, Kenneth. I'll dance on your grave before I'll let you screw with my life again." Felicia stormed out to the echoes of Kenneth's laughter.

NINE

Though in terrible pain, Felicia couldn't get to her car fast enough. She tried to run, but her bruised hip and uncontrollable trembling made it almost impossible. She panted and moaned, eyes darting from side to side as tears streamed down her face. She couldn't believe what she just witnessed – how she was treated. She stood by Kenneth for years, and even after the lies and the cheating, she tried to do the right thing by him, attending his therapy sessions, managing his bill collectors, and even trying to sell the house to pay off his debt to Carmine. She continued to give him the benefit of the doubt, just to get kicked in the head again, and possibly losing Mitchell in the process. Kenneth was so deliberate, so cold, so evil. She saw the man both Jessica and

Carolyn described. What if he hadn't had the accident? She realized she was to be his next victim, and it sent chills down her spine. She felt so foolish, hurt, and angry.

Before leaving the parking lot, Felicia sent a text to Carolyn, asking if Emmanuel could turn his visit into a sleepover. Carolyn was thrilled, but was naturally suspicious. Felicia used the excuse of a headache from the fall, which temporarily took Carolyn off the scent.

Felicia walked through her front door and dropped her keys on the floor. She dropped her purse on the nearest barstool and burned a path to the first alcoholic beverage she could find. Pacing like a caged cat, Felicia gulped wine from the bottle, and relived the conversation with Kenneth. She was done trying to do the right thing. She was finished with logic and optimism. She wanted Kenneth out of her life and the lives of her friends for good. She wanted him dead. Felicia slammed the wine bottle on the counter and grabbed her purse from the barstool. She initially scavenged through the bag to no avail, so she rushed to the sofa and dumped it out. Pens, receipts and accessories of all types spilled on the cushions and the floor. She pushed things out of the way until she found Carmine's business card. She picked up her cell phone from the floor and immediately dialed the number.

"Carmine? This is Felicia Wilson. I want to meet."

"Felicia, what a pleasant surprise. How can I help you?"

"I need to see you. How quickly can we meet?"

Carmine could tell Felicia was upset. "Felicia, it sounds like something is wrong...are you okay?"

Felicia was too upset to explain. "No, I'm fine. When can we meet? Can we meet tonight please?"

Carmine remained calm. "Felicia, I'm not available tonight. Let's have dinner together tomorrow at the diner. I'll see you at 7."

As Felicia thanked Carmine, she heard the front door open. Startled, she dropped the phone and picked up the heavy lead crystal candle holder that rested in the center of the coffee table. She could see the shadow of a tall figure crossing into the family room. It was Mitchell.

Felicia dropped the candle holder. It cracked as it hit the corner of the table, but she didn't care. She ran and leaped into Mitchell's arms, grabbing for his neck and wrapping her legs around him. Mitchell had little time to react – within seconds, he dropped his keys and with feet firmly planted, braced himself for a tackle.

"Oh my gosh, Felicia! What's wrong?"

Felicia began to weep uncontrollably, as Mitchell carried her to the couch. He sat with little effort, while still holding her in his arms. "Baby, what happened?"

As Felicia began to compose herself, she decided this night wasn't going to be about Kenneth. "I'm so glad you're here. I didn't know when, or even if you'd come back. Mitchell, I'm so sorry. I should've handled things a long time ago, but they're handled now, and I don't want you to leave again. I need you."

Mitchell was a little confused, but relieved to hear that progress was made. "I was just stopping by to pick up a client file I left in my room. So, Kenneth knows you're leaving him?"

Felicia had regrouped somewhat and was enjoying the scent of Mitchell's cologne. She began to gently kiss his face and neck. "Yes, he knows it's over. I don't want to talk about him right now."

The combination of Felicia's news and lips had Mitchell completely off balance. He wasn't sure what was happening, but knew he was too weak to fight her off. "Felicia, what are you doing? Where's the baby?"

Felicia began loosening Mitchell's tie and spoke between kisses. "The baby is staying with Carolyn tonight, and if you can't tell what I'm doing, then it's been far too long..."

Mitchell fought his desires just long enough to gently push Felicia away. He wanted to look into her eyes. "Baby, wait...wait a minute. I thought you wanted to wait. Do you know what you're getting us into?"

Felicia wasn't interested in Mitchell's concern, but had to convince him she was. "Honey, I know I've kept you at arm's length during all of this, and you've been amazing. But now that my marriage is officially over, we can be together. I mean, really together..."

Felicia's words were music to Mitchell's ears, but he still felt obligated to profess his feelings. "Felicia, I love you. We haven't really tossed those words around much since we've been together, but I need you to be clear. I do love you, and if you decide you want to stay with me, I will spend the rest of my life making you happy."

Felicia stopped pecking Mitchell's neck and engaged in his stare. She wanted to take in the moment, and respond clearly.

"You carried me through as I discovered my life was a sham. You carried me through when Kenneth came back to life. And now, you want to carry me through the rest of my life. Before we get to that, I have one request."

Mitchell looked concerned, but willing. "What's that?"

Felicia kissed Mitchell deeply, and whispered, "Carry me to bed."

Felicia drifted in and out of consciousness, while morning's light warmed her face. She assessed her surroundings and realized she awoke where she dozed – in Mitchell's arms. Remaining perfectly still, she kept her arms and legs wrapped softly around his broad shoulders and strong thighs. Daylight greeted Mitchell only moments before. He gently caressed her bruised cheek as she rested on his chest, breathing in sync with his heartbeat.

"Good Morning," Mitchell whispered. Felicia purred her response as she stretched and flexed every muscle. Her hip was sore from the fall, but she didn't dare mention it and ruin the moment. Mitchell's hand molded to her arched back then pulled her close, bringing her brow to his lips. She closed her eyes to take in its full intent. As she softly stroked his chest, Mitchell lifted Felicia's chin for the morning's first kiss.

"How do you feel? Are you in pain – I mean, from the fall?"

Felicia touched his cheek lovingly and replied, "No, not at all. This is the best I've felt in a long time. I don't know why we waited for so long."

Mitchell quickly countered, "I do, and we were right to wait. You were trying to do the right thing. Sweetheart, your desire to want to do the right thing is one of the reasons I'm so crazy about you." Mitchell took Felicia's head in his hands and kissed her passionately. "Let's call Carolyn, and ask her to keep Emmanuel until later this evening."

The day moved quickly and after hours in Mitchell's arms, and a long shower, it was time to meet Carmine at the diner. Mitchell insisted he go with her, but Felicia assured him she'd be fine. Mitchell compromised and drove her to the diner, but didn't go in. Felicia arrived first, requested a booth in the back corner, and sat facing the door, eager to see Carmine. After what seemed like an eternity, Carmine arrived. He smiled and greeted the employees and customers as if he owned the place. He strolled back to Felicia, but lost his grin when he saw Felicia's face.

"Felicia, I was surprised to get your call." Carmine slid into the booth. "Is everything okay with you and the baby?"

"No. I mean, yes, we're not hurt or anything." Carmine could tell Felicia was nervous, but allowed her to continue.

"Carmine, I've been a loyal wife and a great mother. I've stood by Kenneth through everything he's done and all the crap he's pulled. And since the accident, I've found out things about him that made my skin crawl. He used to beat his ex-wives, he lied, he schemed, cheated and even told me his parents were dead! Carmine, in spite of everything, I was still there for him. I was going to do the decent thing and make sure he was okay before I moved on, including figuring out a way to take care of you!" Carmine raised an eyebrow, and Felicia realized her choice of words. "I mean, pay his debt to you. I was gonna sell my house. Anyway, I confronted him. He was screaming at me and blasting me for confronting him about his crap! Carmine, he was a monster. He almost seemed demonic. It was the scariest thing I'd ever seen. After I got out and past the fear, I got mad."

Carmine lowered his head, shaking it slowly.

"My my my... This is very unfortunate. I'm very disappointed to hear this. Look Felicia, I'm a businessman. I've worked hard for what I have. But I've been successful without the need to lay a hand on a woman. Touching a woman in any way other than what she requests is the definition of a coward. But I must admit, I'm a bit confused. Why did we need to meet?"

Felicia leaned forward on the table. "I wanted you to look into my eyes when you hear me say this. I don't want me or my son to be a consideration in your future decisions regarding Kenneth. No matter what he tells you, he can't pay you, and I am finished cleaning up his messes. Do what you will to him, but please leave me and my son out of it."

Carmine smirked. "Well, I appreciate you contacting me, Felicia. I wish nothing but joy for you and your son." Felicia wasn't sure if she felt empowered or insane. She had no idea what Carmine was thinking. He wouldn't tip his hand. But she knew it had to be done. She could no longer live as Kenneth's hostage.

"Please allow us to drive you home."

The thought of taking a ride with Carmine was very unsettling. "No, no, thank you. I'm going to pick up dinner here and have a friend drive me home. Thank you, Carmine."

Felicia extended her hand. Carmine took her hand with both of his and kissed it gently. "I have a soft spot for girls. I have daughters."

As he walked toward the door, he said something to the waitress, handed her several folded bills and pointed at Felicia. The waitress looked at the money, stunned, and shook her head eagerly. Felicia knew her meal was paid for, and the waitress's enthusiasm implied he told her to keep the change. Felicia selected her comfort foods, to include a whole peach cobbler.

Once at home, Felicia and Mitchell talked and feasted. She didn't know why, but for some reason, she wasn't as concerned about Carmine as she was prior to their meeting. Mitchell didn't share the same sentiment. He even scolded Felicia for allowing Carmine to pay for the meal.

Mitchell had several long nights at the office ahead of him, and suggested the ladies hang out and keep each other company. Felicia agreed, knowing he didn't want her home alone. Besides, she had plenty of updates for Carolyn and Jessica.

The following evening, the ladies met at Felicia's house. They were thrilled to see the bags of leftovers, but confused when they found out who bought the meal.

"I can't believe you confronted Kenneth AND Carmine! I'm so proud of you!" Carolyn beamed like a proud mother, but Jessica didn't bat an eye.

"Guys, I want him dead," Felicia proclaimed. "I don't want him anywhere near me or Emmanuel, and the only way to guarantee that is, well…" Carolyn and Jessica jumped to attention.

Felicia began her explanation. "Come on! Someday, I'm going to have to answer some tough questions for Emmanuel. It's a lot easier to explain a dead father than a living psychopath. I've never felt this was about anyone in my life, but I'm sure of what I feel."

"Interesting…sounds like there may be a line to knock him off," Jessica mumbled. Both Carolyn and Felicia turned to Jessica with pure surprise. "What did you say?"

"Too much. Let's eat."

"If something happens to Kenneth, the world will be a better place. People get what they deserve. Hell, knowing Kenneth, his sorry ass might outlive us all." The women took a collective deep breath and refilled their wine glasses.

TEN

As the days passed, Felicia didn't do much. She was still a little shell shocked from her conversation with Kenneth. The year was filled with one disappointing discovery after another, but hearing it directly from Kenneth had real a sting. How could anyone be so cruel, so manipulative? And what about Emmanuel? Would he sue her custody? She needed Kenneth to know she would fight him to the death for Emmanuel. Felicia jumped into the shower, threw on some sweats, and headed to rehab center.

As Felicia made her way through the parking lot, she rehearsed exactly what she was going to say. This time, she wouldn't give Kenneth the opportunity to respond. Felicia could see Kenneth's parents through the double doors, leaning on the reception counter. She didn't know they were coming back so soon, then remembered Kenneth telling her about his release. Maybe they could talk some sense into him, and get him to leave her alone, she thought. Felicia didn't mind seeing them again, as long as they took Kenneth with them when they left.

Mr. Wilson met Felicia with an embrace, which completely caught Felicia off guard. "Oh Felicia, I'm so glad they called you. I was going to, but it's been a little chaotic, with all the questions and such. What happened to your face?"

"Nothing. Who called me? What questions?" Mr. Wilson looked confused. He tried to get his wife's attention, but she never raised her head from the high counter.

"Oh, Honey, didn't the police call you?"

Felicia was baffled. "No. What happened?"

Mr. Wilson sighed, "Kenneth was found dead in his room this morning. It's just horrible." Felicia felt her legs tremble, then give way, but Mr. Wilson caught her just before she hit the floor. He dragged her to the row of chairs in the waiting area.

Felicia couldn't catch her breath. "What happened?"

Mr. Wilson sat down beside her. "The police are still trying to figure it out. The morning nurse checked in on him and found him, just slumped over. He had one of those machine cords wrapped around his neck, but they don't think he was strangled, because there was a lot of blood everywhere. Looks like they beat him up pretty badly, then dropped him back on the bed."

Felicia brushed her hair from her face as she stared down at the floor. She couldn't stop shaking. "I can't believe this. I just can't believe this."

Mr. Wilson wrapped his arm around her. "Now Felicia, we'll be here to help you get through this. You won't have to do this alone."

Felicia couldn't cry. She wasn't sure what she felt. "I know, and I appreciate that. I don't even know where to start."

Felicia decided to try to stand. As she rose, a wide man in a grey suit approached. "Are you Mrs. Wilson?"

"Yes."

"Mrs. Wilson, my name is Detective Donald Summers. I'm sorry for your loss. Do you have a few minutes to chat?"

Felicia didn't want to talk with the police until she spoke with Mitchell, but it appeared she had no choice. "Thank you. Um, I just got here, and haven't even had a chance to call anyone. I didn't even know..."

"I understand. I'm sorry, we were just about to contact you. This will only take a few minutes, and then we'll follow up with you later. When was the last time you visited your husband?"

"It's been a few days." Felicia realized her last conversation with Kenneth wouldn't look good to the police, so she chose to only answer what was asked of her.

"I know your husband was recovering from a coma, but do you know anyone who didn't like him, or would prefer that he didn't recover?"

How on earth was she going to answer that question? If she gave names, he'd ask more questions, and there was a real possibility that she was the friend of his murderer. She glanced to her right and looked directly into the face of Mr. Wilson. There was no way she could have this conversation in front of him. "Look, Detective, I'd be happy to help you, but I'm a little stunned right now. Can we please do this later?" Felicia reached into her purse for her keys and turned toward the door.

"That's fine, I understand. I'll give you a call to schedule some time. Mrs. Wilson?"

"Felicia turned back. "Yes?"

"Don't you want to see your husband?"

Felicia paused. She knew she had to choose her words carefully. "No, not like that."

Felicia poured herself into the car. As she sat trembling, her mind filled with images of Kenneth. She flashed back to the day they met, their wedding day, and the first time she saw him after the accident. As much as she wanted to be rid of him, she couldn't believe he was gone. As her eyes filled with tears, she rustled through her purse to find her phone. By the time she had it in hand, Felicia was crying uncontrollably. She decided it would be best to make her calls once she made it home safely.

By the time Felicia pulled into the driveway, she was composed and a little relieved. The ride gave her time to reflect on the bad times more than the good. She walked into the house and could hear Mitchell's voice coming from the office. He was on the phone with a client, so she took advantage of the extra time and opened a bottle of wine. Mitchell heard the noise in the kitchen and wrapped up his call as he headed in to greet Felicia. "Hey Babe. Are you hungry? I was going to..."

"He's dead."

Mitchell leaned in for a kiss, but pulled back before he made contact. "What did you say?"

"He's dead. Kenneth is dead. They found his body at the facility. He was beaten pretty badly."

Mitchell showed no emotion.

"Mitch, did you hear me? Kenneth is dead."

Mitchell responded dryly, "What I heard, is that this nightmare is finally over and we can get on with our lives." Mitchell grabbed glasses from the cabinet and poured the wine.

"Mitchell! How can you be so calm? Kenneth isn't just dead, he was murdered! There was a detective at the facility trying to question me. I know he thinks I'm a suspect. And the Wilsons were there too. There's no telling what his mother said to the police before I got there! This nightmare isn't over – it's just starting a new chapter!"

"Felicia, calm down. The spouse is always a person of interest. It's just standard procedure. There's no telling who killed Kenneth – heaven knows plenty of people wanted to!"

"Calm down? Mitch, there were a lot of people who wanted him dead, but the problem is that I'm friends with some of them! I'm not the only person of interest – there's Carolyn, Jessica, hell, even you!

Mitchell picked up his glass and headed into the family room. "Felicia, you need to drink your wine and relax."

Felicia grabbed her glass and followed. "No, Mitch, I'm serious. Where were you last night? You've been working awfully late over the past week or so. Were you planning something?"

Mitchell spun around and grabbed Felicia's arm. "Listen to me. You have to get a grip! If you start rambling like a crazy woman in front of the police, saying things like that, we will all end up in prison! That sorry bastard is finally out of our lives, and I'm going to pretend I'm sad. Not for one damned minute! So if you want to mourn Kenneth, I get it, but don't expect me to join you. I will be where you need me to be, to help you through the funeral and everything else, but don't ask me to pretend like I'm sad, and don't you dare ask me if I was involved!"

Felicia's eyes were like saucers. She'd seen Mitchell upset before, but had never seen him react like that to anything. Was he involved? "Okay, I won't, you're right. I need to call the girls." Felicia picked up her purse and headed to her bedroom.

"Carolyn, it's Felicia. Kenneth is dead."

"What?"

"Kenneth is dead. Somebody killed him in the rehab facility."

"Girl, you're kidding! When?"

"They think sometime last night, but the police are still trying to figure it out."

"Are you okay? Is Mitchell there?"

"I'm fine – still in shock I think. Mitchell is here, but Carolyn, he's a different person. He's completely calm - there's no compassion at all. When I told him, he didn't bat an eye."

"Felicia, what did you expect? All he knows about Kenneth is how he made our lives a living hell, stole from you, put you in harm's way with criminals and God only knows what else. Mitchell wants a life with you, but he's been in a holding pattern since you two met. Hell yeah, he's calm! He's probably thrilled. You're lucky he didn't break into a jig!"

Felicia paused for a minute. "Yeah, you're right. He just seemed so incredibly cold. And when I talked about us being suspects, he went nuts."

Carolyn became parental. "Felicia, leave that alone. I don't believe for a minute that Mitch had anything to do with this, but if he did, he did it right, and wouldn't leave a trace of his presence. Don't bring suspicion where there is none right now."

"Carolyn? What's that supposed to mean? What are you saying?"

"Felicia, I gotta go. We'll get together later in the week. Let me know if you need help with the arrangements."

Felicia called Jessica. She knew there would be no compassion in this call either, but Jessica needed to know. Maybe it would give her some closure, Felicia thought.

"Jessica, I have news. Kenneth was killed sometime last night."

Jessica didn't say a word. Felicia confirmed the call didn't drop. "Jessica, are you there?"

"Yes, I'm here. I heard you."

"Jessica, are you okay?"

"I'm fine, Felicia. Are they sure he's dead?"

Felicia was baffled by Jessica's question. "What do you mean? Yes, they're sure he's dead."

"Good."

Felicia didn't expect anyone to truly mourn Kenneth, but still had a hard time hearing the responses. She was quickly becoming suspicious of the people closest to her. She thought it'd be best if she tried to rest, and got everyone together for dinner after the dust settled.

After days of calling and coordinating, Felicia finally convinced everyone to gather for a meal and drinks. Jessica was no longer the perfectly coordinated designer diva. Since the death of her mother, she was very casual, in jeans and cartoon tee. She minimized her makeup, (which actually made her more attractive, because she was a natural beauty) and wore her hair in a ponytail. Carolyn was always casual, but had a little extra pep with her ensemble. At first, she tried to show a little compassion for Felicia, but she could only keep the act up for a few minutes.

"Look Felicia, I know Kenneth was your husband – hell, he was mine too...but he got exactly what he deserved, and I'm not going to lose any sleep over it. Now, what are we eating?"

Jessica grabbed the plates from the kitchen. "I agree. I just pray all tracks were covered."

Felicia wasn't sad anymore, but was emotionally drained, and didn't have the energy to debate. "Okay, Carolyn. I ordered Chinese. Jessica, all tracks covered? Have you done something we need to know about?"

Jessica didn't look up. "No. I just don't think anyone should go to jail for this, especially when they've done us all a huge favor. Please, let's eat. I'm starving."

Felicia's focus was no longer on opening the food containers. "Jessica, please tell us. Do you know what happened to Kenneth?"

The ladies settled on the floor around the coffee table. Carolyn and Felicia sat perfectly still, waiting for Jessica to speak.

Jessica took a deep breath and sat her chopsticks down. "After the Wilsons' visit, I was pretty upset. I made a call to an old friend, David Sutherland. He was a guy I'd known for years. We were never in a relationship, but he was crazy about me, and fiercely protective. David knew Kenneth was trouble the first time I introduced them, and tried to get me to leave him alone a million times. I never told him what Kenneth did to me, because David would've killed him. Anyway, we had dinner. We talked a little bit about old times, and I told him that he was right about Kenneth. I told him everything that Kenneth did to me and my mother. I told him I wanted Kenneth to feel what it's like to have someone beating the shit out of him without any possibility of protecting himself."

The ladies were hanging on Jessica's every word. "David told me that his stepfather was abusive and he still remembered his mother's black eyes and bruises. After a few minutes, David excused himself from the table. When he came back, he sat his phone on the table, and told me that no one would ever have to worry about Kenneth laying a hand on them again. A part of me wanted to know his plan, but a part of me didn't care, as long as Kenneth was getting what he deserved.

Felicia gasped. "Jessica, did David…"

Carolyn interrupted, "Oh come on, Felicia! You wanted Kenneth dead as much as we did! The world is a better place with him gone. Don't you ask questions when you really don't want to know the answers. Now shut up and eat."

Felicia countered, "No, Carolyn! I need to know if Jessica knows for sure. I need to know if David had anything to do with it, so I'll know…"

"So you'll know that Mitch didn't? Felicia, you know Mitchell loves you and Emmanuel, and you know that he has your best interest at heart. That's all you need to know. Besides, if you know too much, you could find yourself testifying against people you care about. Leave it alone and eat, Felicia."

Felicia reluctantly stopped asking questions, and ate her food.

ELEVEN

Since Kenneth's death, the days had been stressful and the nights, sleepless. Felicia worked with the parents and funeral home to ensure Kenneth's service had some sense of dignity. Mitchell was supportive and available, but kept his distance when the Wilsons were around.

The funeral director had called Felicia multiple times about Kenneth's clothes, so she decided to take care of it while running errands. She selected a nice charcoal Armani suit, and his favorite black wing tips. The suit still smelled of his cologne. Before it could have an impact, Felicia tossed the suit and shoes on the bed. What a strange task, she thought. Choosing the last outfit someone would ever wear was more of a responsibility than she imagined. What was she going to do with Kenneth's expensive clothes? Felicia contemplated giving them to a local charity, then it hit her – she'd sell the suits and give the money to Jessica to help with her bills from her mother's illness.

In the midst of her grooming, Felicia heard a knock on the door. As she shuffled to the entry, she wondered why the visitor hadn't used the doorbell.

"Hi Mrs. Wilson. I'm Detective Summers – remember, we met at the hospital?"

"Yes, I remember you. Come in."

Detective Summers followed Felicia into the family room. "Nice home you have here. Did you and Mr. Wilson buy it together?"

Felicia knew the interrogation had begun. "Yes. Look Detective, I'm expected at the funeral home soon, so can you please cut to the chase?"

"Mrs. Wilson, you don't seem too broken up about your husband's death. You gotta admit, it looks a bit strange."

"Detective, it would be strange if my husband was a loyal, faithful, kind man, but he wasn't. It doesn't mean I had anything to do with his death. As a matter of fact, I was prepared to walk away without a dime, just to get away from

him. I didn't need to kill him – I could've just ignored him.
That's murder for a narcissist."

"So, what happened with you and your husband? I mean, how
did things go south?"

Felicia sighed, "Look instead of having me rehash my terrible
marriage and missing my appointment, please reach out to
Detective Rodriguez, and ask him to share his discoveries with
you."

Felicia was escorting Summers to the door as Mitchell was
walking in with Emmanuel. Summers looked over to Felicia,
who was mentally scolding Mitchell for his lousy timing.

As Mitchell moved in to kiss Felicia, she blocked him by
reaching over to take Emmanuel from him. "Thank you so
much for watching my son while I take care of the funeral
arrangements. Detective Summers, this is Mitchell Johnson.
Detective Summers is investigating Kenneth's death."

Mitchell stood up straight and extended his hand. "Nice to
meet you. Any promising leads?"

Detective Summers examined Mitchell thoroughly as he shook
his hand. "New leads everyday. So, are you a relative, or..."

"No, just a friend."

"A friend of the family, or just Mrs. Wilson?"

Mitchell didn't appreciate his tone. "What difference does it make?"

Summers raised an eyebrow. "Mitchell, is it? Where were you the night Kenneth was killed?"

"Working in my office, alone."

"Did anyone see you there?"

Felicia shuttered, then interrupted. "Okay, this is going to have to wait. I've got to get to the funeral home. Detective, thanks for stopping by."

Just as Summers stepped out of the house, he abruptly turned back. "Mrs. Wilson, can you think of anyone else I need to speak with?"

Felicia looked out past the driveway, and noticed two men in a black sedan parked across the street, watching the activity. "No, I can't. Goodbye, Detective."

The day of Kenneth's funeral had finally arrived. Carolyn had no interest in attending, so she watched Emmanuel, and Mitchell decided it would be a good day to handle some minor repairs around the house. No one had seen or spoken with Jessica for days. Felicia decided to get the service behind her, so they could spend some real time together.

As Felicia entered the funeral home, she was surprised by the low turnout. Men in expensive suits, and young women in tight dresses chatted in small groups quietly, but no one went near the closed casket or portrait. At one point, Felicia noticed Mrs. Wilson's confused glare while clutching her purse, which gave Felicia a chuckle.

Felicia could feel the stares from the men, and judgment from the women, but refused to acknowledge it. Just as Felicia and the Wilsons prepared to take their seats, a hush fell over the room. When she glanced back, she saw a tall figure with a bald head walking through the crowd, and knew who would follow. Her face felt hot, and hands ice cold. Felicia sat her purse beside Mr. Wilson, and met Carmine in the aisle. "Carmine, thank you for coming."

"Felicia, it's truly my pleasure," Carmine said with a coy smile. "Felicia..."

The funeral director interrupted Carmine's thought. "If you'll take your seats, we'll get started."

Carmine gently touched Felicia's arm, and walked away. Felicia thought Carmine was heading for a seat, but when he got to the back of the room, he continued out the door. His nephew remained, and sat in the last row.

Mrs. Wilson insisted her pastor fly in to perform the service. He struggled as he spoke about this man he'd never met. The congregation's demographic didn't help. As he struggled for words, Felicia squirmed in her seat. How many of the gangsters and mistresses behind her had secrets to share? How much more debt would come to light?

The pastor asked that everyone bow their heads. Just as he got into his praying rhythm, the chapel door opened. Felicia could hear someone walking up the center aisle, and she couldn't resist peeking. It was Jessica!

Jessica looked like she did the first day they met – completely put together. Jessica was adorned in beautiful jewelry, a cherry red silk dress and pumps, white fur cape, and matching hat. Her hair and makeup were impeccable, as she strolled confidently to the front of the room. The pastor's prayer slowly came to a stop as he watched Jessica remove her sunglasses and hand them to the funeral director. Jessica casually slid the colorful bouquet of flowers off the casket to the floor, and plopped her oversized leather handbag where the flowers once rested. The crowd gasped collectively. With both hands, she opened the top half of the casket. The crowd sat in silence. The Wilsons looked at each other, than over to Felicia. Felicia didn't move. Mrs. Wilson dropped her purse to the floor and rose to put a stop to Jessica, but Mr. Wilson grabbed her arm and gently pulled her back to her seat.

Jessica stood in silence, examining every inch of Kenneth's lifeless upper body. Then she reached in and placed her fingers on his neck, slightly under his chin. "Oh my goodness, she's taking his pulse," Felicia whispered. Jessica then lifted Kenneth's arm, and squeezed his wrist, confirming her only desire for years.

Jessica closed the casket, picked up her handbag, and reached for her sunglasses. In full stride, she slid them over her eyes, made her way down the aisle, and out the door.

The room was silent. The pastor's eyes darted from the Wilsons to Felicia, in search of guidance. Before he could receive a signal, a man in a shiny grey suit got up and walked out. He was quickly followed by another man, then another, then a few women. The last person to leave the room was Detective Summers. He gave Felicia a respectful nod, and walked out. Within a few short minutes, the room was empty. Mr. and Mrs. Wilson sat in disbelief, while Felicia worked to loosen the tight bun atop her head. The pastor and funeral director slowly walked over to the rising parents and widow. "In all my days, I've never seen such a thing," the pastor confessed. Mrs. Wilson sat back down, stunned at what she now knew about her son.

The funeral director reluctantly spoke up. "Excuse me, Mrs. Wilson, Felicia - how would you ladies like to proceed?"

Felicia looked at the in-laws, completely lost. She still couldn't believe that a room full of people came to a funeral, just to confirm the guest of honor was truly dead. Mr. Wilson decided it was time for him to step up. "Felicia, it's okay. We'll take care of Kenny from here. We'll take him home, just like we promised." Felicia gave Mr. Wilson a heartfelt hug. She picked up her purse, kissed Mrs. Wilson on the cheek, and finally walked away from Kenneth.

TWELVE

Weeks after the funeral, interest in finding Kenneth's killer died down significantly. Everyone in Felicia's circle was questioned, but released. And since no one was inquiring about the status of the case, the police happily moved it to the bottom of the pile. Mitchell moved in with Felicia, but not before he asked her to be his wife. Life was finally moving in the right direction.

One quiet evening, Carmine reached out and invited Felicia to dinner. Though he made it sound optional, Felicia knew it wasn't. It was time to make things right and pay Kenneth's last debt. Carmine chose a lovely and expensive downtown restaurant, across the street from one of his buildings.

When Felicia arrived, Carmine looked genuinely happy to see her. He gave her a welcoming pat on the shoulder, and helped her with her jacket. "A real shame what happened to Kenneth. I'm sorry for your loss."

"Thank you, Carmine."

"Do the police have any leads?"

"No. Whoever did it made sure they left no evidence. The police said there were multiple blows to the head with some type of large object. That's all they know."

Carmine shook his head. "Interesting... Well, I'm sure they'll do their best to solve this. I'm sure you feel torn about this situation Felicia, but now that Kenneth's gone, maybe you can get on with your life."

Felicia leaned forward. "Carmine, I'm glad you called, because I wanted to talk to you too. I told you before, I don't know the details of your business dealings with Kenneth, and I don't want to know. But I do know he owed you a lot of money. I just need to know what you expect of me. And please, whatever you have to do, please don't hurt my baby."

Carmine frowned, as if Felicia hurt his feelings. "Felicia, I'm not going to hurt you, or your precious son. I really appreciate your willingness to make things right with me. I respect you for that." Carmine paused as he looked away. "I have a lot of respect for mothers. It's the hardest job in the world, with or without a husband. And now that you're a single mom, I can't imagine what you're going through, or what's to come."

Felicia still didn't know if she was being comforted or threatened. "It's not easy, but I love my son, and I want us to have a happy, stress free life. That's why I want to get out from under this debt."

"Felicia, Kenneth owed me a lot of money. If you try to pay his debt, what kind of life could you provide to your son? You could end up with nothing."

"So what am I supposed to do? With all due respect Carmine, I've got nothing else to offer you."

"Felicia, you misunderstand, my friend. I like you. More importantly, I respect you. So, I've made a decision. I decided that Kenneth's debt died with him."

Felicia wasn't sure she heard Carmine correctly. "Wait – what? What are you telling me Carmine? I don't have to pay?"

"The debt was Kenneth's, not yours. Don't get me wrong, I have many associates that have family businesses - you know , the wife is a part of the business. I have a very different arrangement with them. But you weren't involved in this. You've already paid in so many ways. Besides, Kenneth's friend Lucas will ensure I get reimbursed fairly, through both cash and services."

Before Felicia could thank him, Carmine lifted his menu in front of his face. "You know what I love here? The lamb. The lamb is delicious."

"I'm sure it is. I've never had it."

"Oh, you must have it tonight. Melts in your mouth. They serve it with very few sides so you can savor the flavor of the meat. You know what makes the meat so tender?"

Felicia was amazed at how easily Carmine changed the subject. "No, I'm not much of a cook."

Carmine rested his menu on the table. "They tell me the best way to ensure a tender leg of lamb, is to tenderize it a bit while it's still frozen."

Felicia was lost and had no idea where the conversation was going. "I don't understand."

"Have you ever seen a whole leg of lamb?"

"No – I don't think so...well, maybe."

"Not the ones in the grocery store. I'm talking the ones hanging in the back of the butcher shop. It's an interesting shape, kinda like one of those big clubs they say the cavemen used to carry around. Narrow at the shank, wide at the thigh."

Felicia remembered that everything Carmine shared thus far had a purpose, so she paid close attention.

"In the old country, our families didn't have all of the kitchen utensils and appliances you have now, so they would take the leg of lamb or whatever piece of meat they had, and bang it up against hard objects. Rocks, the side of the house, you know, whatever could take it."

Felicia was getting uncomfortable, and she thought it might be a good idea to leave before he changed his mind about the debt. "Yes, that's interesting Carmine, but I really can't stay. I need to pick up my son."

Carmine's relaxed tone changed. "Make arrangements for Emmanuel. This lamb has to be eaten as soon as it comes off the grill."

"Carmine..."

"So my grandmother, Camille, she loved my grandfather, but he was a real son-of-a-bitch. He was a drunk, didn't take care of the family, and was known to put his hands on her from time to time. I could tell she was getting fed up with him slapping her around, but what could I do? I was just a kid.

So one night, after thirty years of marriage, my grandfather came home drunk. He pushed my grandmother into a wall and she cut her head on a kitchen shelf. He demanded food, and she knew what she'd get if she didn't feed him. He poured himself into a chair at the kitchen table while she pulled a beautiful, small frozen leg of lamb out of the big icebox she kept in the back of the house. My grandmother was pretty strong for such a tiny lady. Eight swift blows to the head. He never saw it coming. She was finally free, and her lamb was tenderized. She seasoned it, and while it cooked, she dragged my grandfather out of the kitchen and buried him in the vineyard behind the house. She told me all about it on her deathbed decades later, but she told me with a smile on her face."

Felicia couldn't move and wasn't even sure she was breathing.

"You know Felicia, some people don't believe in Karma, but I absolutely do. And no matter how hard you try, you can't plan when Karma's gonna visit. Karma never knocks. You could be sitting at your kitchen table, or, say, in a rehab facility, and Karma walks through the door. With just a few quick blows, her job is done, and a beautiful meal is provided."

Felicia broke into a cold sweat. She couldn't speak.

Just then, the waiter appeared with a platter of beautifully cooked lamb and a plate of asparagus with baby potatoes. Carmine took his napkin from his lap, and placed it on the table. "Felicia, I've got another appointment, but I want you to sit back and enjoy a good bottle of wine and this beautiful meal. I had the lamb tenderized especially for you." Carmine stood and buttoned his suit coat. "It has been a pleasure knowing you. By the way, your home is paid off. Keep it, enjoy your son, and have a good life. Oh, and tell your lovely friend Carolyn I'd like to call her sometime."

Felicia wondered when Carmine saw Carolyn, but it was low on the list of the night's discoveries.

Carmine kissed Felicia's hand with parental affection, and casually strolled away through the sea of tables.

END

Made in the USA
Middletown, DE
30 March 2023

27962243R00090